EARTH WOLF & FIRE

Eliza Falls book 2

MAGGIE FRANCIS

a magical smalltown romance

EARTH, WOLF and FIRE

Eliza Falls book two

Maggie Francis

COVER DESIGN: JM Design
DEVELOPMENTAL EDITOR: BookMarten Editing Services
COPY EDITOR: Amy Ollerton

Maggie
FRANCiS
✦ magical small town romance

www.maggiefrancis.com

For G
Despite it All

For A&H
Always and Forever, no matter what

Tate

The crash of boxes falling in the back room makes me pause as I close the door behind me. I cock an ear, letting my Wolf suss out how worried I should be. The hiss of whispers and a familiar growl settle my hackles, and I chuckle. Shaking my head, I drop the package I've brought with me and pocket my keys. I still feel chuffed they gave me a set for the shop, a sense of pride washing over me as I look around the space. Big windows and warm light woods make the space feel welcoming, while thoughtfully arranged inventory- a lot of it handmade- makes the shop feel more like an extension of your best friend's kitchen, inviting and comfortable. Speaking of, I pull my phone out of my back pocket just as another scuffle and a grunt comes from the back room, and I chuckle again.

"Don't destroy the inventory this time, you horny assholes!" I call out. My brother, Seb, can usually tell when someone approaches, but if Cora has him distracted I can sometimes sneak up on him. Although, from the sounds of things back there, I don't want to see whatever they're getting up to. They had to reorder a whole shipment of teacups a few months ago when they knocked a box off the back shelves in their *enthusiasm*.

I turn on the stereo behind the front counter to drown out my brother and his Mate and text Desi.

TATE: **Hurricane Sebra is currently destroying the back room. Send help.**

DESI: **Just ignore them, they won't break anything this time!**

TATE: **You coming in this morning?**

DESI: **Look up Buttercup!**

I look up from my phone and see my girl Desi cross the street in front of the shop through the large windows. She's a ray of Godsdamned sunshine and I'm reminded again of how lucky I feel that she's my best friend. We'd fooled around a little bit last year to see where it could go, but we're too alike to make it as romantic partners. Maybe she knows more than she lets on, but as far as I can tell, we're better off as friends. And luckily, we're both excellent communicators so it never gets weird.

I tuck my phone back into my pocket as I walk to the front door and open it for her. She's got one arm loaded with bags and a travel tray of drinks from the cafe across the courtyard perched on top while she wrestles her phone into a pocket of her long cardigan.

"Good morning sunshine," I smile as she walks past me to put her loot on the counter.

"Good morning, my Two Bite Brownie," She replies, stretching up to kiss me on the cheek. We easily organize all the stock she brought in with her and line it up behind the counter while we wait for Cora and Seb to resurface.

"They'll be at it for a little while longer," She says breezily. "Want to pop over to Butter My Muffin before we open the shop? They made those almond cookies you like this morning."

"Hells yes I do!" I drum my fingers along the top of the counter and give her a little bump with my hip.

We stroll over and order a baker's dozen of my favorite cookies, still warm from the oven, and I watch Desi laugh with the owner while I shove a few into my mouth at once. My eyes roll back in my head and I groan out loud.

"Sela, you need to marry me and have my babies."

Desi and Sela both laugh at my antics as I lick the crumbs off my fingers before digging into the bag for another one.

"Seriously, I don't know what kind of kitchen sorceress you are, but these cookies are magical."

Sela is a beautiful, half Japanese woman with smooth gray hair that she wears in a braid down her back while she's at the bakery. Which is pretty much all the damned time. Our town keeps her busy in the kitchen, whipping up all the treats you can imagine. Her husband works the front till most days and they're always rosy-cheeked and smiling.

Sela laughs at me again and puts another six cookies into a paper bag for Desi.

"As much fun as that may be, you rascal, I imagine my husband would disapprove."

"What would I disapprove of Sela my Dearest?" Walter booms as he lumbers into the front of the bakery.

Walter's a giant of a man with a long red beard and ruddy cheeks. His voice is deep and craggy, and he has the softest heart when it comes to his Sela. He leans down to kiss the top of her head and nods to Desi and I as he straightens to his impressive height. He has to be at least six foot seven, and if I didn't know how gentle he is, I might feel a bit nervous.

"Tate wants to marry your wife and have cookie babies with her." Desi sings up to him. Walter snorts and kisses his wife again.

"That's a reasonable desire, she's an angel. But unless she's changed her mind, only I will be making cookie babies with her."

"Walter!" Sela tuts, smiling up at him with flushed cheeks. "You naughty old fart. Whatever will I do with you?!"

Walter just dips her for another kiss, which she happily returns. Desi and I call out our thanks again and leave them to their romance. Watching Sela and Walter so tender and effusive sends a pang of longing through my Wolf. They have an enviable love that's easy to see, and I smile to myself.

"This whole town is full of lovers, have you noticed?" Desi says sweetly to me. Her shiny copper curls are tucked up into a messy braid which she's wrapped around her head, and her long skirt swirls around her calves as we walk back through the courtyard to the shop. Desi is a beautiful woman, and I smile and wiggle my eyebrows at her. Something in the water of this goofy town keeps all of its occupants giddy in love, and I love it. My Wolf is just as romantic as I am, and we both secretly hope that we'll find our forever too.

"Do you need to find yourself someone special, Desi girl? I know we decided we're better as friends, but you know I *lurve* you and we can give it another try if you need to be satisfied." I give her my cheesiest grin and a wink. She laughs up at me and rolls her eyes.

"As much as I thoroughly enjoyed myself, Big Turk, I love you too much like a brother now." Her eyes sparkle at me and I feel my Wolf preening. He's always loved Desi, but she's right. It isn't the intense love of a Mate, like what Seb and Cora share. Those two are on a whole other level. Desi and I are tight and will always have each other's backs, and that feels good and right to my Wolf and I. Desi is as much Pack to us now as Seb and Cora are.

Seb and I have been roaming in a tidy little pack of two for the last few years before we made our way to this weird town a couple years ago. Our family pack has always been small, just our grandparents and us. There are a few photos of other family members that I recall from the walls of Gamma's kitchen, faded old pictures of people I don't remember meeting, and a few of my parents, but they left when I was too small to remember them other than vague sensory memories. My Wolf likes to have more Pack around, so the addition of Cora and Desi makes us feel a little easier in our skin. I'm a social animal and M'Ladies fill a gap I hadn't realized was there before we met them. The bond between Cora and Desi is almost as strong as the Mate Bond, so when Cora finally accepted my brother, I got two new sisters at the same time. Anyone that Desi falls in love with will likely be Pack too. After the proper hazing and initiation of course. I'm not going to let Desi fall for an asshole, and Cora would skin both Seb and I alive if we didn't defend her honor. Mate Bond or not, Desi is Cora's ride or die, and Cora is *terrifying* when she gets pissed.

"It's just so nice to see so many people around us feeling the flush of love, don't you think?" Desi says. We've made it back to the shop and Desi pauses, her head tilted to one side as if she's seeing something out of the corner of her eye.

"Oh good, they're dressed!" She rattles the keys in the lock a little more than necessary, just in case. Once we're back inside the shop and have deposited our spoils on the counter, I call out to my brother.

"Oi Lothario! We brought sustenance!"

Seb rolls out of the back room, running a hand through his messy hair. His cheeks are pink and he doesn't make eye contact with Desi. He has no problem glaring at me though. I laugh and clap him on the shoulder as he settles next to me and pulls out the cookies.

Cora practically oozes into the room behind him and bites her lip when she glances at Seb, looking embarrassed. Her eyes are shiny and her shirt is inside out. In a move so smooth it could have been a magic trick, Desi brushes her hand over Cora's back and snags the lacy panties that hang out from the hem, and tucks them into Cora's hand.

"Ohmygods Desi! Thank you! I couldn't find them when we were getting dressed and had a mini panic attack thinking that they'd show up in someone's mail out." Cora laughs and shoves them into her back pocket, blushing.

Seb looks anywhere but at me and I chuckle.

"Don't you guys get enough of each other at home?" I tease. They moved in together nearly a year ago, shortly after they finally got over their damn selves and got to getting down. But they still moon at each other like horny teenagers and it's adorable as fuck.

"Shut up, Tate." Seb growls at me, even as he crosses over to Cora and runs his fingertips across the back of her neck. She shivers and bites her lip again and I have to roll my eyes at them. I feel the subtle brush of Seb's Wolf sending calm confidence through the pack bonds and I smile as my own Wolf tucks his tail.

"I think it's swoony and dreamy. You're gonna eat your words, Tate O'Connell. Just you wait." Desi croons at me.

I look over at her. Desi's gifts as a Spirit witch mean that she sometimes gets glimpses of the future. Premonitions that are never wrong. Was this something she's seen? Do I have a Mate in my future? My Wolf pushes closer to the edges of my skin in eager anticipation, and I feel his hopefulness. I give myself a little shake and tell myself to chill. Werewolves are long-lived and even if there's a Mate in our future, she might not cross our paths for years and years. My life is good. Great even. I love my jobs, they're very different but they keep me feeling busy and satisfied. I have a great place to live behind my kooky Aunt Jett's place, and the best Pack I could ever want. I don't need to worry about stumbling into a Mate Bond anytime soon. I'm only twenty-seven for fucks sakes! I have years of living ahead of me before I settle down.

2

Ulla

I love the feeling of the earth beneath my feet. The squelch of mud or the soft press of moss. I carry my shoes in my hand as I wander slowly through the clearing. My poor mother would cringe if she knew I was barefoot. It drives her mad when I shake my boots off the first chance I get, even to this day. But I remember these woods. I haven't been here in years, but as soon as I stepped off the path and started meandering, it all came back to me. The little waterfall that sings over that ridge, its clear, chiming laughter ringing out for everyone to hear. But that's just it, isn't it. No one else hears it. Just me. And I haven't confessed that to anyone since the third grade. Not since the kids had teased and taunted me about it after I told them that the trees on the edges of the schoolyard whispered to me. Little kids can be so mean.

They probably don't even remember how hurt I was when they laughed. Or when the third grade Queen Bee viciously corralled some other kids into laughing with her. That haunted me for *years*, until I switched to a correspondence school.

I was always the weird kid. The girl who's too quiet to talk to humans but loves to talk to trees. Or animals, or rivers. It doesn't matter how much I try to tune it out, the earth is always around me and her children always speak to me. But after all those years of being the odd one out, I've become the woman I am today. And while she's not the most popular or perhaps the most confident, I'm practicing loving her all the same.

Sighing, I continue to wander aimlessly through the McLaren Wood Provincial Park. This place has been special to me ever since I was a little girl. My parents made a point to do family trips every summer to some incredible nature preserve, national park, or magical camping spot. We'd spend our summers traipsing through forests, climbing rocky valleys, or splashing in swimming holes all over the place. It was heaven. For a kid who was more at home outside than in, these were formative and life–affirming seasons. And it's here that I finally had friends. My summers here were full of the only friends I really had growing up, making Eliza Falls the first place that felt like home. We've kept in touch through the years, childhood penpals that became true adult friendships. I'm looking forward to seeing them and reconnecting, but I haven't told them I'm back yet. With our adult lives getting busier over the last few years, our correspondence has become fewer and farther between. We've been texting here and there lately, but I've been away so long this time I'm looking forward to surprising them when I finally make my way into town. This past week has been all about settling in with my parents and decompressing after my years in the city.

The woods here have become some of my favorites. There's an energy here that's always felt like home to me. Something about the air feels *right*. Like this is where I'm meant to be. The leaves in the tree directly above me shimmer and whisper in my ear.

"I know, I thought so too." I reply softly. The trees here are more talkative than the last time I was here. I close my eyes and let their welcome wash over me.

Spring here in Eliza Falls feels like an enchanted dream. The woods practically sparkle with the energy of the place and it fills me to the brim. When Mom decided she was ready to retire and settle down here last year, I couldn't get myself packed up fast enough. It took me a little longer to get all my ducks in a row, but as of last week, I'm back in my parent's house. I didn't need to move here with them, I'm 26 and have lived alone for the last five years. But when they told me they were thinking of moving *here*, to this place I can't stop dreaming about? It was a no-brainer.

I shiver as the wind picks up a little bit, and it hums against my skin.

"You're right, I should head back"

I stretch my arms over my head, shaking some of the dirt from my shoes into my hair as I do.

"Oops! I forgot about my shoes again." I laugh at myself and bend over to toss my hair out. It's so blonde, the dirt will be really obvious and Mom'll give me hell about it when I get home. Straightening myself to my full height, I turn around to head back.

My folks bought a little Cape Cod style house with a wrap-around porch and an actual tree fort in the back-yard. Mom had squealed with delight when she saw it the first time, and before they'd even finished unpacking, she'd taped paint chips all over the front porch. Dad's holding strong so far, but it's only a matter of time before she paints the entire house a bright, sunshine yellow. It's her favorite color and she's had a vision of this house floating around in her mind for as long as I can remember.

As I wander back towards the south parking lot, I trail my hands over the branches of all the trees and bushes I can reach without straying from the path. Salal and salmonberry are looking lush and verdant, and I tell them all how beautiful they are this time of year and how happy I am to be back with them again. I pick up a few fallen branches as I go and have collected a sizable bouquet by the time I get back to my little car. Humming to myself, I tuck them into a bucket I keep in the back for this very purpose. I pour the remains of my water bottle onto an old towel I have stuffed into the bucket. I left it back there after I had Dad's pet snake with me the other day. She's a lovely ball python that someone had brought to my dad to stuff, but was very much *not dead*. He didn't have the heart to give her back once the original owner made it clear they had no interest in a live snake. My dad's a real softy when it comes to animals, so his choice of profession as a taxidermist is ironic for the man who rescues every creature that crosses his path. I've seen him tear up over a lot of the animals he works with in his studio. He works with museums all over the continent, preserving animals and generally nerding out over every single one of them.

He named the snake Suzanne before he told Mom he was planning to keep her. Luckily Mom is an open-minded woman. She and Suzanne are friendly, if not overly cozy. And because I'm currently living with all of them right now, Suzanne is also my friend. She and I have been snuggling on my mom's fancy chaise lounge all week while I read in the sunshine. She's not overly affectionate, but snakes generally aren't. However, we've developed an understanding and she tolerates us all well enough. We both enjoy soaking up the sunshine, and she'll tuck herself around my shoulders for a nap when I'm home and relaxing. Dad went a little overboard on her terrarium situation and she has two of them to choose from. After I got settled last week, she wanted to feel the forest on her scales, so I'd brought her out for an afternoon adventure on the first really warm spring day.

Mom is a (newly) retired costume designer for stage and screen. Growing up I never lacked dress-up opportunities. I was surprised the first time I slept over at my aunts and realized that boned corsets and human hair wigs weren't the usual costume bucket treasures for other kids. She has a flair for the dramatic, which could be considered embarrassing if she wasn't also so utterly charming and welcoming. She's just my mom, and trying to dim her light isn't worth anything as mundane as embarrassment. Her best friend, my Aunt Alma, is one of the reasons they moved here to Eliza. And the two of them together are a tropical storm of shenanigans and laughter.

As I pull into the driveway an hour later, there's a commotion coming from the backyard. I hear raised voices and a soft, unexpected yipping. I grab my bag from the seat next to me and pull my treasures from the back hatch so I can put them in water once I get into the kitchen. The cool morning wind tousles my hair around my shoulders, and I ask if I should worry. The sense I get is amusement, so I continue on into the house and head through to the yard to see what my parents have gotten themselves into.

After settling the branches I collected into one of Mom's big kombucha brewing jars, I quietly pad to the back deck to see what they're arguing about. Mom looks exasperated, her arms crossed over her chest, foot tapping in aggravation. Dad's holding a bundle of something in his arms that wiggles and I see a little nose poke out and sniff the air. Making sure to not inadvertently take a side by

12

standing too close to either of them, I take myself to the top step of the deck stairs and sit down. Immediately, the little bundle in Dad's arms starts thrashing around and he can't hold it safely anymore. He crouches low while he exclaims over it.

"Whoa little buddy, you'll hurt yourself! Here you go, here you go." A tiny red ball of fluff scampers directly over to me and throws itself into my lap.

"Abe, I swear, we cannot keep that! Ulla, Honey, do not get attached!" My mom practically hollers to the yard in general.

But it's a lost cause. Because burrowing into my lap is the littlest, softest, cutest baby fox I've ever seen. He's so small that he can't possibly be properly weaned yet.

"Daaaaaaad, why do you have a baby fox?" I squeal. Oh, this is my childhood all over again! We often had rescues we'd nurse back to health before releasing into the wild. Looking down at the little nugget in my lap though, I know this one isn't going to be released.

"Don't you dare imprint on that animal, Ulla Jolene!" Mom grinds out. "We already have Suzanne to deal with and a fox isn't a domesticated animal!"

"Oh Katrin honey, just look at that little guy." My dad pleads. "His mama was brought in by a hunter and they were going to leave him to die. He can't defend himself, he's just a baaaaby." There are tears in my dad's eyes and I can tell that Mom knows this is a fight she can't win. Both Dad and I are already in love with him and Mom throws her hands up in the air in frustration.

"Dennis is a sweet soul Mama, he's going to be no trouble, isn't that right little one?" I croon at the little baby. He's snuffling around in my lap, rooting around for food.

"DENNIS??!!" Mom shrieks.

I know his name is Dennis because he told me. He

looks up into my eyes and I'm a goner. I listen to my parents continue their conversation and hear that Dad is going to fortify the tree house into a den of sorts for the kit and Mom is slightly appeased. I think she knows on some level that Dennis will spend more time in her bed than she's willing to admit. Once my dad and I get invested in a rescue, all bets are off the table and we get a little intense. But she's settling down for now and I gently scoop Dennis up into my arms and take him inside. He burrows into my shoulder and tucks his tiny nose into my neck.

"Oh buddy, let's find out what a baby fox needs to eat," I whisper into his soft, spicy neck fur.

A quick internet search later, it turns out foxes eat a lot like dogs and cats do, so I put in a call to the local pet store. I order some organic raw meat and they recommend some supplements we can blend into it to make a mash while Dennis is still so small. We'll have to take him to the vet and make sure he's alright. But his eyes are bright and clear, and now that he's settling into my arms, falling asleep, I can see that other than a little dirt, his fur is thick and healthy.

Dad comes inside and sniffs when he sees the sleeping kit.

"Oh my girl, he's a sweet one, isn't he?" He says softly. I chuckle as I pass the snuffling Dennis over to my dad.

"I called the pet store and they've got some food set aside for him. Do you want me to head into town and pick it up?"

"Clever girl. Yes, I want to stay and snuggle him. Your mom is on the warpath though, so give her a wide berth until she settles down. I think she'll come around on this little guy pretty quick though, just *look at him*." Dad gazes down at Dennis with hearts in his eyes and I'm reminded again that this little kit is now a part of the family. Mom has a lot of bark, but not a lot of bite. She'll see how invested Dad is and accept Dennis sooner rather than later. She loves my dad's soft heart and secretly enjoys the drama of the strays he brings home. She has to put up a fight though or we'd be overrun. Laughing softly, I kiss my dad's cheek and scoop up my bag from the back deck. Mom is on the phone with someone, hissing in frustration. Then she snorts a laugh and rolls her eyes and I guess she's talking to Aunt Alma. Mom's best friend is a dramatic and engaging jewelry designer who dances in and out of our lives regularly. This is the first time in their lives that they'll live in the same place since they were in their twenties and they're both ecstatic about it. I'm thankful for Alma's influence on Mom's decision to move here too. This funny little town holds such a big place in my heart and settling down here feels so good.

3

Ulla

I have a big bag of goodies for Dennis slung over my shoulder and a book about red foxes tucked under my arm as I stroll through town. Gail, the owner of the pet store, is a font of information, and my mind is reeling a little from all the suggestions she had for feeding a rescued fox kit. She told me there's a rescue and rehab center on the outskirts of town I should contact, and waxed poetic on the man who runs the foster program. Her gaze had gone a little glassy when she started talking about him, and she even blushed at one point; that made me smile to myself. Perhaps she'll do something about that blush. It seems to me that she's a lovely person. I hope she works up the courage to connect with this Tate guy. From the way she tittered about him, he sounds like a catch.

I pass the entrance to a little courtyard that's lined with shops, and I can smell the most amazing blend of fresh bread and cinnamon. I slow my steps and take a few deep breaths in, savoring it. The new leaves in the trees around me rustle encouragingly and I smile to myself.

"Why not indeed. I could use a cuppa." I turn myself

around and step slowly into the courtyard. It's a clear, early spring day, and the sunshine is bright overhead. The café has patio umbrellas set up and there are big pots of lemongrass spaced evenly throughout the open space to deter the bugs that come with this sweet warm weather. Lights strung between the awnings connect the different shops, while a few tourists with their guidebooks and locals alike are mingling and enjoying the mid-morning sunshine.

A soft breeze tickles my ears and I look over to the right. There's a lovely display in the shop window with snake plants and Queen Anne's Lace, a variety of beautiful pottery and what looks like tins of loose tea. I wander a little closer and look at the rest of the display.

While I'm staring at the different herbs, imagining how they blend together, a doorbell chimes and a musical voice calls my name.

"Ulla! My sweet Starlight! You're finally back!" I swing my head up in the direction of the voice and look at a golden Goddess of a woman smiling at me as she approaches. Her strawberry copper hair is braided in a crown around her head, and she's wearing a long dress that slips around her curves. She's beaming at me, and I have to blink a couple of times to clear my head.

"Desi?!" I cry, suddenly breathless. Desi is one of my summer playmates and a dearest friend that I've been looking forward to reconnecting with. I haven't told her that I'm in town yet, as I was hoping to surprise her, but she's turned the tables and I'm the one feeling surprised. I'm so happy to see her that I nearly drop my bag. She grins at me as she sweeps me into her arms and hugs me tight.

"I thought I'd see you earlier today, but I see you got sidetracked! Katrin will come around, my Moonflower, Dennis will win her over in no time."

I laugh at her keen insight. I'd almost forgotten that Desi always has a sense of what's going on, but it seems like her gifts have sharpened since we were teenagers. I haven't seen her since we were both nineteen, the last time my family had come to town for the summer.

"I'm glad to hear that." I smile at her. "Mom is pretty incensed right now."

We laugh together and she releases me from her wonderful hug.

"Why don't you come into the shop and say hello to Cora, she's just in the back *'reorganizing the Autumn inventory'* again." She wiggles her eyebrows at me as she throws up finger quotes and I press my lips together in a grin. Desi often drops hints in subtle ways and I'll find out soon enough what has her eyes twinkling this time.

"I'd love to. I can't believe it's you! I'm so glad I stopped to smell the bakery," I say as we walk together into the shop whose window I was just staring at.

"Wait, this is your shop? I was so wrapped up in the window display I didn't look at the shop sign!" I exclaim. Cora and Desi had talked about their dreams for a shop together when we were teenagers.

"We did, my Vixen Princess. Come inside and see how wonderful it is." She winks at me and hugs me again before taking my bag and book, placing them behind the front counter. I can't help but smile at her. Desi is a ray of sunshine and always has been. We met when we were eight. Cora is Alma's daughter, so we've known each other like cousins, but I hadn't met Desi until that summer. We were all at the beach, Cora glaring at the water like it had ruined her birthday. Desi had boldly walked up to me and my parents and solemnly informed us that she was my very dear friend and we needed to build a sand castle to cheer up her grumpy mermaid as she tossed her head over at

Cora. My dad chuckled at the scene and my mom indulged her, telling us to stay close. I'd meekly followed Desi over to a furious Cora and the three of us were inseparable every summer for the next eleven years.

Shaking my head at the memory, I look around me and take in the dreams of my dearest friends. Cora and Desi are the closest thing I have to sisters and the only true friends I had growing up. The kids at home were predisposed to exclude me after I'd been branded as a weirdo, so I was often left to my own devices. But after that day at the beach all those years ago, I had friends. Delightful, offbeat, forever friends.

I feel very lucky to have found them when I did. Being a social outcast so young was challenging to navigate on my own. My parents always did their best, supporting me and never stinting on their love for me. They'd tried to have children for years before they adopted me, and I've never sensed they felt anything other than true joy and love being my parents. I'm their daughter, and that's that. But there's something transformational about a best friend, a companion that chooses you and sticks with you, because they love you and grow with you. My miserable school months were offset by the heady joy of friendship that I've never taken for granted. Growing up here every summer with these two women, who chose me to be their friend when we were children, filled in a lot of the cracks left behind by the ostracization I experienced during the school year.

The summer I was twenty, I decided that I needed to do some soul searching. My magic has always been a part of my life, but as I got older, it became more unpredictable and harder to control. The way nature responded to me was interfering with my daily life and I found that the best way to control it was to push it down and away inside of myself. I stayed away from Eliza Falls for years, because it's here that my magic feels the strongest. There's something about this place that settles me and makes me let down my guard. I thought I needed to stay away in order to feel some control over it, and because of that choice, I've missed out on so many little details. Now that I'm back, hopefully for good, I'm looking forward to catching up on everything I've missed now that we're together again.

The shop is a feast for the senses in a clean and orderly way. The whole space feels like a perfect blend of the two women I love so much, and I feel a moment of regret for allowing myself to drift away from them for so long.

"I'm so proud of you Desi, it's more beautiful than I could have imagined!" My voice cracks a little, the feelings overwhelming me.

"Oh don't you go fretting Starlight, you were busy and had to find your own path back to me."

Desi bumps my shoulder with hers and I smile gratefully up at her. She always knows.

"I'm still sorry I lost all that time with you. Tell me everything you guys have been up to!"

At that moment, the back door swings open and a very tall hulk of a man walks out and nods to Desi and I.

"Seb, Darling, this is Ulla. She's back and we're keeping her."

"ULLA?!" The shriek comes from behind the mountain of a man standing in the doorway. A flurry of grunting, arms and pink hair swirls around him and skids to a halt in front of me.

"Cora!" I cry and we jump into each other's arms and hug each other tight. Now I'm crying and laughing, both women surrounding me as we all talk over each other and are generally a gaggle of raised voices.

Seb smiles and leans against the counter, letting us have

at it while we reconnect. We've stayed in touch over the years, but the last few have seen us all so busy with our lives that our correspondence naturally slowed down.

"So wait, you came home to a fox kit and your dad already has a rescue snake??" Cora asks with raised eyebrows.

"Well, to be fair, Suzanne came with them from home. She's been on the scene for a couple of years now." I reply, taking a sip from one of Cora's sample tea blends. It's soothing and minty, with an undercurrent of something floral. Lavender maybe? I don't care what's in it, it's heavenly.

I laugh at Cora's grimace.

"She's actually really chill. She spends a lot of time sunning herself in one of her elaborate terrariums. You know how my dad is. Once he brought her home he spent days researching how to build her the best nest and honestly she's pretty sweet. He's working to install heated floors in the new house for her. Mom got on board once she realized that Suzanne was eating the mice that sneak into the kitchen."

Desi gives me a small smile and I blink at the gleam in her eye.

"Starshine, you should take your Dad to meet Tate."

"Oh yeah?" I ask. "Who is Tate? This is the second time someone has mentioned him today."

"My brother." Comes a deep rumble from Seb. He'd been quietly working around us in the background while the three of us sat on the floor catching up, absorbed in each other. He's got a quiet, confident energy that skates across my senses like a hug. Cora beams up at him.

"Tate runs the volunteer program at the animal reha-bilitation center on the outskirts of town. I bet he could hook up your Dad with all sorts of helpful tidbits for Dennis. Great name by the way."

I chuckle and finish my tea.

"He named himself. I can't take any credit for that." I respond, still smiling. Seb glances over to me at that, and I cringe. Even after all this time of hiding my nature, I'm so comfortable around Desi and Cora that I forgot that Seb doesn't know me. He's been so quiet that I let my guard down.

"This is a safe place, Moonflower," Desi says softly when she notices my expression. "Seb knows about our gifts and it's all good." She looks at him pointedly and he blushes and ducks his head.

"I, ah, have my own secrets." He says, practically a growl. He looks uncomfortable for a moment but then shakes his head. He glances at Desi and she nods.

"She's one of us, Seb, it's cool."

Sighing, he relaxes his shoulders and takes a deep breath. "You can tell her then. I trust you, Des." He ambles back towards the storage room, presumably to let us keep chatting without him, and I wait patiently. I can tell he's uncomfortable, and I know the feeling. Sometimes it's better to not see people's reactions to things. I imagine, since he's engaged to Cora, that he's used to how unusual things can get around her sometimes.

Cora watches him go, her gaze hungry while she stares at his backside. I giggle at that, and she turns around blushing.

"Just how long have you guys been together again?" I tease.

"Coming up on a year now." She sighs dreamily.

Desi and I both laugh at her dramatic swoon and Cora smiles at us. I'm incredibly curious, I want to hear everything I've missed, but I don't want to push. I know what it's like to have secrets and I'm not going to force the information. If Cora is safe and happy and Desi trusts him, then it doesn't matter what he is.

Cora's still smiling when she speaks softly.

"Seb's a werewolf, and my Mate."

I blink. Well. I'd definitely been getting a growly vibe from him, but other than that I wouldn't have guessed. Weres, shifters in general, are pretty rare. Almost as elusive as vampires are in the supernatural community. Us witches are practically a dime a dozen compared to how often you run into a shifter. I take a slow breath and think about it. I've never met a Were before, but considering I have my own nature-based magic, I certainly can't judge. I think again about how happy Cora clearly is and how decidedly not worried Desi is and that settles it for me.

"Cool. I've never met a Were before. He seems lovely and intense." I smile as I say it and Cora snorts.

"Yeah, intense is right."

"All I care about is that you're safe and happy. Plus the way he looks at you is pretty dreamy!"

Desi chuckles and rolls her eyes, "StarBlossom, you have no idea of the smoldering looks these two toss around. It's delightfully annoying."

Cora tosses a smug look in Desi's direction and stands up.

"I need to do a few more things to get the store ready to open. We sorted out the mess in the back, so I'm going to start on the opening checklist."

Desi grins at her and then looks at me.

"Cora and Seb have had to *reorganize* the back storage room several times now," She says, whispering conspiratorially.

"Oh?" I look at Cora and see she's flushed a sweet pink that matches her hair.

"Mmm hmm!" Desi sings. "True Mates have a hard time keeping their hands to themselves it seems." She's all glittering affection and Cora rolls her eyes at her. Clearing her throat, Cora reaches down to help me to my feet and pulls me into a fierce hug.

"I'm so glad you're back, and this time for good," She whispers into my ear.

I return the embrace and feel warm contentment flow over me.

"Our Fairy Princess is where she needs to be." Desi says from behind us before elbowing herself between us and turning this into a group hug. I laugh again, unable to stop smiling now that I've reconnected with these two women. It really does feel like I'm where I'm meant to be. Finally safe to be myself, free of the judgment of narrow-minded peers. I take a deep breath, taking in my two friends, returned to me after such a long separation. But knowing now that it hasn't changed anything between us. Perhaps nothing would.

4

Tate

I haul another bale of hay off of the back of the truck. Old Pete had dropped it off this morning, and I want to get it all unloaded before lunch. I spend a fair amount of time these days helping out at General Pawspital, the animal rehab center that serves our town. My Wolf isn't a problem here. He's an asset when we have animals come in who are injured or scared because he can sense what they need and give them that energy. Being able to soothe a terrified animal and help the team gives us an immense sense of satisfaction.

Working here with the animals balances out my role running the administration side of O'Connell Bros custom carpentry. My social nature allows me to comfortably market and advertise Seb's quieter skillset. We've both been working with our hands since we were pups and Gamma had sent us off to wheedle attention out of Granddad. He's more of a loner than the rest of our small family pack and spent a lot of his time woodworking or repairing old cars in his big back garage. Seb and I spent hours out there once Gamma realized it soothed our Wolves to be close to Granddad. He's such a cool old grump. Now that I think about it, he and Seb are cut from similar disgruntled clothes. Only Gamma can coax a smile out of the old coot most days. I'm pretty sure he got a kick out of us pups once we stopped getting into everything and he'd taught us enough to allow us to sit still in there with him.

Those skills serve us well now that we run our own carpentry business. Seb and I have always worked really well together, but it wasn't until we moved to Eliza Falls that we started working for ourselves legitimately. Starting our own carpentry business is a natural fit for us and something that happened really smoothly. Shortly after we moved into Aunt Jett's old carriage house, she'd asked us to do a couple of odd jobs around the property in lieu of rent. While we were getting our feet under us that had worked out in our favor. Once word spread about some of the custom builds we'd done for her, the neighbors started hiring us to fix or rebuild bigger and bigger projects until we were doing it nearly full time. We rented a big workshop in town with a little showroom, and the rest is history. Seb's a genius when it comes to woodworking. He can see the wood becoming something beautiful before we even get started, so I follow his lead in most of our projects. I manage all the accounts and advertising, making sure that we stay relevant and as busy as we'd like to be. We both build, working on projects that use our muscles, allowing our Wolves to settle into the physical labor. It's soothing to use our hands to make a living. But here at the rescue center, being able to let my Wolf out a little more and stretch his legs a bit, I feel at ease and of service. It's a heady combination that I don't take for granted.

Once I get all of Old Pete's hay cleared out of his truck

bed, I wipe the sweat off my face with the bottom of my shirt. I wander inside the main building of the center to check in with Mel and see if she can use me with the animals today. I often take some of the dogs home with me in a foster situation. Being a Werewolf allows me to support a lot of the more aggressive cases in a more efficient way. Once they realize I'm higher in the pack than they are, we usually have no trouble. It doesn't often take long for most animals who come in to realize that they're safe and where they stand once my Wolf makes an appearance. Mel's human and she thinks I just have a way with animals. She threw a lot of *Crocodile Dundee* references at me when I first started working here and I'd had to watch it to finally get it. She isn't so far off base, although I don't have to squeak or growl while pointing my pinkie and thumb at them to make it work. Usually just letting my Wolf close to the surface settles everyone down pretty quick.

I chuckle as I walk past Old Pete flirting awkwardly with Mel as she stands at the front desk. He isn't even really that old, probably in his late fifties. But that's what everyone calls him and he never corrects us. I wink at her as I walk behind Old Pete and waggle my eyebrows at her. She rolls her eyes at me and laughs at something that Pete says. They're well suited. I should ask Desi if she knows anything about them.

I walk into the back office to grab my canteen from the fridge, and my Wolf sharply snaps to attention. I blink and straighten, stilling myself so he can take point on our senses. Something ripples over my skin, an electric pinging that shoots straight up into my scalp. I shake myself and tilt my head to catch any new sounds. Moving on silent feet, I walk slowly back towards the front desk.

My Wolf starts to rumble low in my chest, a deep

purring I've never felt before. He's scented something new, something *incredible*. It's like moonlight and rain and spring-time and sunshine all at once. I take a deep breath in, letting the scent wash over us and soak it in. I want to roll around in it. Swim in it. What is this??

Mate.

My Wolf is pushing close to the surface now, trying to get closer. We need to see whoever smells so fucking good. I've never felt him yearn before, but that's what this feels like. A reaching. Striving. He needs to get close. But we're surrounded by humans on all sides and I have to play this cool. Whoever it is, is supernatural, that much at least I can tell from here.

Holy shit, my Mate is out there. Who the hell can it be?? I know everyone in this weird little town. How can our Mate have been here and we didn't notice? That doesn't sound right. In all the stories I've heard, the Mate bond is something that happens immediately. Jesus, poor Seb took one look at Cora and he was a goner.

I take another deep breath to try to calm my Wolf down before we step out into the main room of the center. A woman I've never seen before is quietly walking up behind Old Pete. He's still chatting up Mel and they haven't noticed her come in. She's petite, probably only tall enough to come up to my armpits. She's… *breathtaking.* Her skin is soft brown and flushed pink across her cheeks and shoulders from the sun. She has a halo of white blonde hair that practically floats around her shoulders in soft curls, pinned haphazardly off her face with a couple of flowers. She has actual flowers in her hair. The contrast of her moonlight hair against her brown skin is strikingly beautiful. Her eyes are dark, deep pools of midnight. She's soft all over, gloriously curvy hips flare out from an hour-glass waist and smoothly sumptuous calves that flow down to dainty, delicate, bare feet. She holds a pair of sandals in one hand, and as I watch her, she slows her steps and slips her shoes back on.

How is she real? Where did she come from? She looks like a pixie princess just wandering in from the forest. My Wolf rolls over inside me. He wants to be closer to her. We watch her glance around and blink suddenly, tilting her head as she looks past the front desk. Drew, one of our regular volunteers, hurries out of the back kennel area where some of the larger dogs are exercised. A huge beast of a familiar dog lumbers after him, the lead loose behind her.

"Oh shit, Mel! I tried to get her back into her kennel, but she gave me the slip!" Drew hollers as he runs past. He tries every time he comes in to work with Daisy, this particular dog, and she runs roughshod over him every time. Every. Single. Time. I admire his persistence, but I don't think this is a battle he'll ever win. Daisy's a real sweetheart, but she's enormous and stubborn as hell. We expect she'll end up staying here with us at the center for the rest of her days. She's just too much for most people to handle. She won't hurt anyone, but because of her size and the way she approaches you, suddenly and enthusiastically, she often knocks people over. I start to run as I watch her head straight for the woman. *My Mate.* But as I start to sweat that I won't be able to get there in time, I watch her smile softly at the giant dog running right for her and put her tiny hand out towards Daisy. She says something to the dog, though I can't hear what, over the thundering of my pulse in my ears. And I watch, dumbfounded, as Daisy dances to a stop and sits down right at my glorious Mate's feet.

This all happens in seconds. Mel, Old Pete and poor Drew all watch agog as this little slip of a woman smooshes Daisy's face into hers and scratches her behind the ears. Daisy's practically drooling all over herself at the attention. The woman looks up at me then, blinking her big dark eyes, and I'm lost.

5

Ulla

W hen I leave Desi and Cora's shop, I decide to swing by the Rescue Center and check in to see if they have anything I can bring home for Dennis. Reconnecting with my childhood friends has been such a wonderful experience and I'm so grateful my parents came back here when Mom retired. I'd hoped I'd see Desi and Cora, but it's been so long since we've actually been together, I wasn't sure how it would go. Years of text messages aren't the same as really connecting with people, and I worried I'd been away for too long. But it's like I never left! I feel all of their love swirling around me as I drive out to the center, and I'm already looking forward to seeing them again.

I park my little car in the dusty lot and grab my shoes from the passenger seat. I only wear them when I absolutely have to. Mom still can't understand why I want to feel the earth under my skin. But it's just something I need to feel grounded. A literal connection to the earth and a way to be closer to the elements. Managing my magic can get tricky; the voices are often loud, and I've found over the years that this helps. Dad doesn't love it, but he makes sure to leave me a soft towel by the door. This way we can appease Mom a little by not tracking dirt through the house.

I carry my sandals in one hand as I cross the grass to the center's main doors. It's a large compound that covers what looks to be a few acres of woodland, with fenced-off areas neatly maintained behind the main building. I listen to the wind as it caresses the hair around my neck, and I'm pleased to hear the animals here are well cared for. The residents inside are all calm. The trees surrounding the center titter sweetly all around me and I get a sense of anticipation from them. Something's coming. Perhaps an early summer storm is brewing. I make a mental note to mention it to Dad, as he'll want to make sure the tree house is secure before we see any intense weather. Although we all know there's no way that little kit will be sleeping in the treehouse anytime soon.

Chuckling to myself as I quietly make my way up the steps and into the building, I look around. I take in the information they have pinned to a bulletin board placed to be seen as you walk in. Adoption notices and posters for lost cats are tucked in next to wildlife warnings and an old Smokey the Bear ad.

There's a middle aged man flirting with the woman at the reception desk. She smiles warmly at him as he leans a little over the counter to lower his voice towards her. I smile as I lean down to put my sandals on. As I straighten up, I hear a joyful rumble and a scrabbling of something that sounds… large. And fast footsteps. I glance over to see a lanky teenage boy dash out of a back area. He's all elbows and long legs churning as he races in front of the biggest dog I've ever seen. I listen to the creature lumbering after him, her voice full of mischief and joy to have gotten the upper hand – again, by the sounds of it! I grin as I watch it all unfold.

"Oh shit, Mel! I tried to get her back into her kennel, but she gave me the slip!" The boy cries as he runs towards the front doors. I send a little nudge towards the enormous dog and she shifts direction straight for me. I keep smiling and raise my hand towards her.

"Slow down, pretty girl, I'd like to say hello properly," I say softly under my breath. I don't need to raise my voice for her to hear me. She prances prettily as she gets closer and then drops dramatically at my feet. Her big brown eyes gaze up at me and I laugh as I grab her head and give her a good scritch behind the ears. Oh, she's a drooler!

"What a lovely girl you are, aren't you, Daisy Girl?" I croon at her as she smears dog saliva all over the sandals I just slipped back on. I feel eyes on me and look up to see the couple from the front desk and the boy near the door all staring open-mouthed at me. And a Man. With a capital M.

Good heavens, where did *he* come from?? He'd managed to get close to me as I'd been loving up on Miss Daisy here, and I hadn't noticed. Well, I'm noticing him now. Holy shitballs, this man is gorgeous. My gaze travels up, up, up his impressive form, glistening with an earthy sweat. Tall and broad without being too bulky. He has bronze skin and golden hair, like he spends hours in the sunshine. And glittering hazel eyes that are currently deep diving into my soul as he stares at me. He's breathing heavily, as if he'd just been running. And he smells like a spicy dream, woodsy and dark, but also bright somehow. Citrus?? Like he rubbed a fresh orange peel across his sandalwood skin under a hot summer sun. My throat goes dry as I blink up at him while I absently continue petting the dog. He clears his throat, his bright eyes never straying from mine.

"Are you alright? Daisy here can be a bit overbearing sometimes." His voice is raspy and deep. It sends a thrill over my skin, and I have to swallow before I can speak.

"I'm fine, thank you. She's a lovely girl. She's quite fond of this place." I say. My voice is breathy and I blush as I watch his eyes darken, pupils stretching wide. Something flashes behind his gaze and I startle. There's something else watching me from behind his eyes. Something bright and vital and *primal*. *Someone* else.

"Oh!" I whisper. "Hello to you too."

He inhales sharply and blinks at me. Oh Gods, I've done it again! I spoke without thinking and now I feel exposed. He takes a step toward me and I press my lips together as I hold my ground. My breath shudders back into my body as I look into this beautiful man's eyes and see a *Wolf* looking back at me. This is… new.

"Hello, little one," He growls. *GROWLS*. Oh. Oh *wow*. It's the voice of the Wolf inside him! Like a spell breaking, the other people in the room, the people who've probably watched this whole exchange, filter back into my consciousness. Daisy pushes her big body into my hip and I stumble back a step. The incredibly hot Wolf man reaches out and softly grabs my elbow to stop me from falling over, and my skin feels seared where he touches me. Smoldering heat licks up my arm and I feel my whole body wake up. Hello indeed.

"Thank you." I breathe as he lets go of my arm, although he doesn't retreat. He stays close to me as the woman comes over and gently takes Daisy's lead from where it's laying on the floor. The dog woofs deep and low, then licks up the woman's arm as she extends it out to me.

"Goodness, what a way to say hello!" She smiles at me

as I shake her hand. "I'm Mel, the director here, and I'm *so sorry* about Miss Daisy here. As you can see she's very sweet, but her big body tends to do some of the talking for her." Mel reaches down and pets Daisy, true affection in her smile. Daisy scoots her big body closer to Mel and leans against her instead. Mel locks her legs in place and manages to stay upright against the big dog's weight.

I look around and see that the older man has left during the commotion and the teenager is wringing his hands behind Mel. I smile at him and he steps closer. As soon as he does, I feel a rumbling behind me. I'm surprised to realize it's the very attractive man standing close to me, his front nearly pressed up to my back. I tilt my head and listen to the Wolf that's inside him. I've never met a werewolf before today, but what else can he be? The Wolf is feeling possessive. Of me? Huh. This is a plot twist I didn't see coming! I turn my body slightly so I put the man at my back into my line of sight and smile up at him. I send calming thoughts to his Wolf, and watch as his eyes turn their intense gaze from the boy back to me. As I watch, he blinks and relaxes his shoulders. He takes a deep breath and shakes himself a little. A subtle reset, but a necessary one. This young boy is no threat to them, and I get the sense that this possessiveness isn't something they've dealt with often. Hmm hmmm hmmm. Curiouser and curiouser.

I smile more freely at him and turn back to Mel and the boy.

"I'm so sorry Ma'am, I lost my grip on her leash and she took full advantage." The boy's pleading eyes are full of apology.

"Oh it's no trouble, she's utterly lovely. Aren't you, Sweet Girl?" I sing down to Daisy. Her big tail thumps against the floor and she gives us all a slobbery grin.

"Drew, Honey, why don't you get Daisy here back out to the yard so she can get some of her energy out, and then you can start lunch for the rest of the crew back there," Mel speaks kindly to the teenager. He nods and takes the leash from her hand and clicks his tongue at Daisy. The two of them make their way back down the hall that must head to the back of the center's main building, and the three of us watch them go. Mel turns back to me then and puts her hands on her hips.

"So what can we do for you today, now that some of the excitement has passed?" She asks me. She looks at the man behind me, who still stands very close to me. So close that I can feel the heat pumping off of his big body, and his bewildering scent is all around me, making my head spin. Her eyes narrow and she clears her throat pointedly. I choose to ignore the sexy inferno behind me for the moment, and I lace my fingers in front of me.

"I came in looking for someone named Tate to ask about fox kits. My dad came home with a very young one this morning and we want to make sure we care for him properly."

The aforementioned hot mountain of man twitches behind me. Mel tilts her head a little and after glaring at the man behind me for a second longer, she turns back to me.

"A fox kit? How did he stumble across the little guy? Is it visibly injured?"

"Oh, no, Dennis is just fine. He was hungry and scared but otherwise he looks good. My dad is a taxidermist and hikers or hunters bring him animals from time to time. I think Dennis' mother was brought in early this morning and they didn't know what to do with the kit. My dad's a real softy and scooped him up. This isn't new for him. The strays I mean, the fox is a new one for us." I chuckle.

"Taxidermist, you say?" Mel looks at me thoughtfully.

"That's right. My folks moved here last year. We used to visit when I was a kid every summer, but when Mom retired they decided they wanted to settle here."

"I'm familiar with Abe. He's been talking about you joining them here for the last little while. He's pretty excited to have his girls under the same roof again. Welcome to Eliza Falls officially." She smiles at me and I grin back. Her energy is genuine and warm and I understand why she's a great fit to lead this rescue center. She makes you feel calm and welcome.

"Tate honey, why don't you take… I'm sorry, I didn't wait for your name!" She grins ruefully at me.

"I'm Ulla."

"Ulla, a pleasure to meet you." She nods towards Tate again, the man still vibrating behind me.

"This here is Tate, he's pretty much our animal whisperer. Tate, Honey, why don't you take Ulla to the kitchen and put together a newborn carnivore supplement package for her to take home."

6

Tate

Ulla.

My Mate's name is Ulla.

My Wolf is beside himself inside me. His joy and satisfaction are palpable and I have to work hard to reign him in so we don't overwhelm her. I roll her name around inside my mind. Ulla. *Oooooh-la.*

She's a Goddess. An aspect of Artemis surely, the way she calmed Daisy down so effortlessly. The way she spoke directly to my Wolf?! How *did* she do that? How does she even *know*?! I'm reeling from all of this. Not only have we found our True Mate, something I hadn't expected to happen so soon, maybe even ever. But she's also some kind of magical Wolf whispering, Goddess-like creature who speaks directly to my Wolf?!

Holy fuck.

Be cool man. Don't get weird. Weirder. This is already weird as fuck.

Mel wanders off after giving me another sharp look. I'll be hearing about this later. I'm usually a lot smoother than this. Hell, I'm chill and cool. Unruffled. Unflappable.

Consider me officially flapped right now, because I can't bring myself to move away from this pixie of a woman standing in front of me. I can barely even look away from her.

She turns around to face me. We're standing so close, I can see the flecks of silver and gold in her dark irises. Her hair smells like wildflowers, sunlight and sparkles. Do sparkles have a smell? What the fuck is happening? How can she *smell like sparkles*??

"It's nice to meet you, Tate." She says softly. So softly that I'm sure no one else could've heard her. Does she know I have my Wolf's sharp hearing? Or is she just this soft spoken? I have no idea what to say or do. I just stare at her. Oh fuck, why can't I say anything? Is this what Seb felt like all that time? How the hell did he survive all that? She's been standing in front of me for maybe fifteen minutes, and I'm craving her skin like a drug already.

No wonder he was such a bloody grump all the time.

My Wolf is stretching himself to get closer to her, his yearning feels like a physical force reaching out of me. Oh Gods, this is intense.

"Would you feel more comfortable if we went outside?" Ulla asks, tilting her head to one side. How long have I been struggling in front of her? Wow, dude, this is a great first impression. Her expression is calm, no evidence of freaking out – that I can tell. My Wolf starts rumbling inside me, frustrated with my hesitation.

"Come on then," She says. She very softly touches my forearm. It jolts me out of my trance, and I shake myself again.

"I'm so sorry, I… yes, let's go outside." My voice sounds gravelly like I've been on an overnight bender. She gives me a serene smile and turns around. Her dress floats around her like we're in a slow-motion Jane Austen moment, and I can't resist reaching out to her. My finger-tips brush against the ends of her cloud-like hair and I feel my chest clench tight.

Oh holy mother of dragons I'm fuuuuuucked.

She walks ahead of me on light feet, hardly making a sound at all as we cross the grass. She's heading directly for the trailhead we use for some of our dog walks. I continue to stare at her, soaking up as much of her with my eyes as I can. She's just so… *lovely*. Everything about her is soft. Her voice, her hair, her curves. Oh shit, I'm staring at her ass. I tear my eyes up to the sky. My Wolf is purring constantly and his desires are blatantly clear. I'm desperately trying to keep my physical reaction to her to myself, because she *just met me*, but my cock does not care. At all. I grind my teeth together and try to think of anything that might defuse the situation.

Dog farts.

Cleaning toilets.

Aunt Jett's chickens.

Nope. Fuck. I can't do it. She's too close, too real.

I clear my throat and try to catch her attention.

"Um, Ulla?" I manage to grit out.

She turns around and looks up at me. Her eyes are like pools of midnight and I stutter step to a stop in front of her.

"This is an unexpected turn of events, isn't it?" She asks.

"What?"

"Meeting like this. I had a sense that something was going to happen soon, but I figured it was going to be more mundane, like a storm. The birch were gossiping when I got here." She chuckles in chagrin then. "And now I'm telling you about the trees talking to me. An auspicious beginning."

I grin at her. She's smiling wryly back at me, and I realize she's a little bit awkward. I've been so wrapped up in the nearness of her, and the magic of her, that I hadn't noticed yet that she looks nervous. She's curling and stretching her fingers over and over, and she pulls the corner of her bottom lip into her mouth. It makes her bottom lip pout out on the other side and that makes my Wolf practically howl inside me.

She blinks and startles, "Oh!".

Then she tilts her head to the other side and her eyes look a little unfocused. A bit like Desi does actually, when she's having a vision.

Is Ulla a Spirit witch too? Is that how she knows about my Wolf?? I hold my breath. We're just inside the edge of the woods behind the center now, still on the path but out of sight of the main buildings. We're alone until someone comes walking along the path and I know we don't have anyone volunteering to take the dogs out on a nature walk until this afternoon.

Plus my Wolf will know before anyone gets close.

"Um, should we just be honest with each other? I can tell he has something to say." She finally says. Her voice is so soft, like chiming bells or songbirds on the wind. Oh, here we go. I'm thinking in poetry. This is getting ridiculous! My Wolf chuffs, laughing at me, and her whole expression changes. Her eyes glitter in the light shifting through the tree cover and her smile is blinding.

"He is, isn't he?" She laughs in her delicate, low voice, and I groan.

"Are you talking to my Wolf right now? Are you guys in on a joke?"

She looks up at me then, her gaze sinking deep into mine and her smile slowly fades. Her breathing changes, her lips parting slowly. I can feel my own gaze getting darker and my Wolf isn't laughing anymore. He's purring and she gasps.

"Oh wow, this is intense," She whispers. "I've never had a conversation like this before."

"Like what?" I grind out. My neck and shoulders are getting hot and my dick is straining against the zipper of my jeans.

"Hearing your words and his thoughts at the same time. He's just as clear in my head as you are in my ears. Oh! Goodness! That's rather forward, wouldn't you say?" She's blushing. Her cheeks flooded the most tantalizing shade of pink and her eyes grow darker. My Wolf is prowling inside me, sending me images of what he wants us to do, how he wants us to claim her, and I try to lock that shit down.

"Oh!" She gasps again, and covers her cheeks with her small hands.

"Ohmygods, that's very sexy, oh dear!" She bites her bottom lip again and laughs a little nervously. "Um, perhaps you should ask me out on a date first?"

I bark out a laugh and run my hands through my hair. Her eyes track the movement and I can smell her arousal.

Well then.

My Wolf is very pleased. He's fucking preening inside me and I watch her gaze go a little unfocused again and then she chuckles.

"Keeping secrets from you is going to be tricky, isn't it?" I ask her.

"Very." she replies simply. "I don't do it on purpose, I promise. His thoughts are just very powerful."

"Obnoxious is more like it," I grumble. But it's half-hearted. My Wolf is as much a part of me as my heartbeat and we're on the same page when it comes to this ethereal creature in front of us. Ours. She's ours. But, while she seems to be taking my Wolf in stride, which is fucking unexpected, I'm not going to push the True Mate thing at her just yet.

"Hmm, is that a Wolf thing?" She asks suddenly.

"Huh?" I blurt, not realizing she's picking up on those thoughts. This is going to be harder than I thought. How the hell is she getting all of this?

"The Mate business." She replies, seemingly unconcerned.

"Who *are* you?" I whisper.

7

Ulla

There are so many voices swirling around in my head right now. Tate's Wolf is growling and preening, practically shouting his joy at me. It's adorable and terrifying at the same time. I'm getting whispers from the trees and wind around me too, making it hard to hear my own thoughts in all of the noise. Maybe strolling into the woods isn't the best idea after all. I'd hoped to get a little space to wrap my head around what the Wolf is telling me, but the tittering of all the other voices is making it hard.

Hard like the bulge in Tate's pants. Oh good gracious, that's also making it difficult to think straight. This is all happening so fast! How is it possible that this golden God of a person is looking at me like that? He's so beautiful. And so big. Oh my heavenly stars, he smells like my dreams, all fir trees, fresh air and masculine spice. The Wolf chuckles again at my appraisal and I shiver. I try to breathe around the ache in my belly, but the feeling drops lower and heats my core. Tate's eyes are bottomless and hungry. I want to sink into them.

"I, uh," my voice is scratchy, the way he's looking at me sends my thoughts spiraling into dirty, *dirty* places and I'm not sure I want to claw my mind out of the gutter just yet. I clear my throat and try again.

"I'm just me, nothing particularly interesting to see here," I say, aiming for nonchalance. It comes out squeaky. Ugh, this is ridiculous. I'm not a seductress and I'm definitely not smooth. Only one thing for it.

"I can hear animals in my head," I say in a rush.

"You can talk to animals?" His brow furrows and Gah! Why does that have to be so sexy too?

"Do you wear glasses?" I blurt out.

"What??"

Oh Gods, Ulla! *You ridiculous nincompoop!* I can't believe I said that out loud. Oh no, more words are coming. Shut up shut up *shut up!*

"Sorry, I was just thinking about your frowny eyebrows and that you'd probably look amazing in glasses, like a sexy professor or something. And then I thought about how it would make me feel to watch you frown over a tricky passage in an old scroll or something, and now I am picturing you as Indiana Jones."

Oh for crying out loud the words won't stop!

"And then what if I came in with more research and we couldn't fight the tension between us? And you suddenly realize my hair has fallen loose, and you take off your glasses and then tuck a strand of my hair behind my ear. And because we're in the middle of a mission to beat the Nazi's we can't act on the feelings and we have to fight against our instincts and how sexy that would be and ohmygods *please say something to shut me up!*"

"Indiana Jones, huh?"

I blink, cringing, and try to sink into the ground.

"Ohmygods." I groan as I cover my face with my hands and wish for a time machine to take me back to a land that exists before my verbal unicorn poop ramblings. I feel his rough fingertips on my hands as he gently pulls them away from my face. A flare of heat zings all the way to my toes and I kick my sandals off again. Wiggling my feet into the moss feels good. Cool and grounding and like I can almost breathe again.

Tate waits patiently while I take a few deep breaths to get my racing thoughts under control, and when I look up at him again he's grinning, lopsided and adorable and I'm in a lot of trouble.

No. Not in trouble. I'm looking into the eyes of a Werewolf whose Wolf is shouting *"Mine"* joyfully at me over and over again and I'm not in any trouble at all. Yes, it feels like I'm reverting into a horny teenager and my palms are getting a little sweaty just thinking about it. But I'm also feeling the rightness of it. Like a puzzle piece clicking into place. Or like coming home after a long trip away.

"So, what does this Mate business entail?" I ask him. "Are you my werewolf boyfriend now? I mean! Oh jeez, that's weird, I'm sorry! Of course you're not my boyfriend! I mean… unless that *is* what this means?? What does this mean? I just don't know what to do here!"

I'm babbling again.

He chuckles softly as he lets me ramble myself out. He's going to think I'm an unhinged stalker-type person.

"You're taking this pretty well for someone who didn't know me from Adam an hour ago." He says. He watches me with avid eyes. Searching my soul, maybe? I press my lips together and try to calm my racing heart down. Am I taking this well? I think about my life up until today. I've always been an outcast, always the weird kid. It was only here in the summers, when I had Cora and Desi, that I was ever really a part of a group. And I hadn't been here in years. My job at the library back in Vancouver kept me busy, but other than a few casual friends at work, I don't really feel connected to anyone. Maybe part of what's making this feel ok and not giving me the screaming meemies is that it feels nice to be wanted. To feel like I belong to something. To someone.

Even if that someone is a complete stranger who's also a werewolf. A sexy as hell werewolf, whose Wolf is shooting pervy thoughts straight into my brain. Hoo boy! Or am I just rationalizing this complete absurdity because I'm a hopeless romantic and this feels like it's straight out of a romance novel? All my time spent reading Charlotte Bronte, Jane Austen and Johanna Lindsay is rearing its dreamy head.

"Um, well, I don't get Serial Killer vibes from you."

The Wolf huffs a breath at me, and I feel his outrage. Tate smiles ruefully at me and ducks his head.

"Yeah, I guess you can hear him pretty clearly huh?"

"I can," I reply. Knowing Tate's true feelings about things through his Wolf is reassuring. I can tell they aren't lying. Wolves don't lie, that's a human thing.

"Is this not how it usually works?" I ask him. Is this because of my gifts, I wonder? Are other Were Mates unaware of their partner's natures?

"I don't think so?" He says, but it comes out more like a question. "My brother is Mated, but his Mate didn't know for a long time. She can't hear his Wolf like you can hear mine. It was actually pretty funny to watch them glare longingly at each other for nearly a year. Seb isn't a great communicator." He chuckles as he says it. I can feel his Wolf's amusement too.

"Oh of course! Cora's Seb. He does seem like the strong and silent type."

"What? You know Cora?" He looks shocked. "Didn't you just move into town like yesterday?"

"Well, last week yes, but I've known Cora and Desi since we were kids. My family used to summer here when I was little. My mom and Cora's mom are old friends from art school, back in the eighties. I just haven't been back for the last five years or so. I ran into them in town this morning when I was getting some food and supplies for Dennis. Their shop is so beautiful! It felt so good to catch up with them, and Seb was there with Cora. Desi teased them about reorganizing the storage room again." I smile up at Tate.

He smiles back down at me. Oh Lords, he's really pretty.

"So," I start again, clearing my throat. "Mates don't usually hear each other's thoughts, but since I can hear animals, I can hear your Wolf?"

"That seems to be the case." He replies.

"Does that bother you?"

He looks thoughtful for a moment, while he squints at me. His Wolf grumbles a muffled something or other, sounding peeved, but I can't hear what he's thinking. I smile up at Tate.

"Are you trying to hide your conversation from me?!" I laugh.

He groans and shakes himself out.

"Did it work?" He asks.

Laughing, I swing my arms a little. "Kind of? But your poker face needs some practice."

He chuckles then too, and tilts his head to the side, still looking at me with a shrewd gaze.

"Let's get some of those newborn carnivore supplements and then go get some lunch?" He looks at me, waiting for my answer. I nod and start walking back along the way we came. Tate walks quietly beside me, his heat pulsing against the thin fabric of my dress. I want to reach over for his hand but that feels like more than I can handle right now. This whole morning has been a whirlwind of surprises and I'm going to need some time to wrap my head around it all.

8

Tate

Once we've collected the supplements for her dad, we head back outside towards the parking lot and I follow Ulla to her car. I stay close to her the whole time, my Wolf not allowing me to give her any more space than totally necessary. He's puffed up with satisfaction over her. Her easy acceptance of the situation has me baffled, but my Wolf just purrs his contentment. I'm not ready to leave her side yet either, so when we get to her car, a tiny hybrid with the back seats full of books, I pause and take a deep breath. Her scent invades my senses, and I groan softly. She smells so damn good.

She turns around and studies me. My Wolf watches her intently, while she takes us in quietly.

"Tell me something about yourself, please," She says in her soft voice. I roll my shoulders back and purse my lips. Her gaze travels to my mouth and a delicate flush moves down her neck. I like the thought of making her blush, and my Wolf rumbles low in my chest in agreement.

"Something that *isn't* sexy, please." She says with a raised eyebrow.

I chuckle and press my lips together to suppress my grin. She smirks up at me while she waits for me to speak.

"I moved to town almost two years ago with my brother. We own and run a custom carpentry business and up until Seb and Cora worked themselves out, both my brother and I lived with our Aunt Jett." Ulla leans her small frame against her car while I speak, crossing her arms in front of herself. She tilts her head a little as I finish.

"Wait, I think I've met your Aunt Jett!"

"Yeah?" I'm not surprised, our town is a small one and Jett is a busybody. I bet she bustled herself over with something homemade as soon as Ulla parked her car on her first day in town. She laughs with her wind chime voice.

"She knocked on our door a few days ago and brought a jar of homemade apple butter and a scarf for Suzanne."

"Your mom?" I ask.

"Oh, um no, Suzanne is a ball python. Dad saved her from a client a few years ago who wanted to stuff her."

"Wait, what? Like someone brought your dad a *live* snake and expected him to kill it and then stuff it?" I'm aghast. Who does shit like that?

"Yeah, my dad has met some weirdos. But he wouldn't do it and the client wasn't interested in keeping her unless she was stuffed. They said Dad could deal with her before storming off. She's really lovely though, and once my mom got over the shock of my dad coming home with a four-foot-long python in a box, they made her as comfortable as they could." Ulla shrugs like it's totally normal to have a snake as tall as a third grader show up at her parent's house.

"Does your dad bring home exotic animals often?"

"Hmm? Oh, all the time. My mom had to put her foot down ten years ago after he came home with a badger. He wasn't as friendly as some of the others and he tore up a whole loveseat one afternoon while I was at school. Dad made friends with a wild animal rescue organization after that, and now Mom keeps a 'Non-Acceptable Animals' list on the fridge."

She must have experienced stuff like this all the time because she doesn't seem the least bit phased by the information she's telling me. Maybe this is partly why she doesn't seem worried about finding out that she's a Werewolf's Mate, or how she can hear my Wolf like he's in her head instead of mine.

"Sounds like you had an interesting childhood," I say. Her eyes look a little pinched when I say that. I wonder if maybe it was interesting, but not as nice as she would have wanted it to be.

"You could say that." She replies quietly.

"Will you tell me something about you now?" I ask her.

She holds my gaze as she considers it. She bites the corner of her lip again and I barely contain my Wolf's growl of desire. She blinks and inhales sharply.

"Whoa Buster, this is going to take some getting used to." She breathes.

She clears her throat, then speaks with her husky mermaid voice.

"I'm a librarian, although I don't have a job lined up since I moved here. But my contract in Vancouver ended recently and I've always loved the woods around Eliza Falls, so I took the chance to come here and see where it would lead me. I'm staying with my folks right now."

Oh fuck me, she's a *librarian.*

My eyes roll back into my head and I clutch the car next to her, literally swooning.

"Tate?!" She calls out. It sounds like it's coming from far away.

My name on her lips makes my Wolf howl hungrily in my chest, and I lock my knees so I don't fall over.

"Will… will you revoke my borrowing privileges, Miss Ulla?" I croak out.

"Oh, you ridiculous jackass!" She grits out at me as she slaps me in the stomach.

"Oof, not so hard!" I grunt. Her smack is surprisingly strong for her tiny frame.

"I thought you were about to pass out!"

"I still might." I grin down at her. "The sexy librarian is my favorite fantasy."

"I'm an unemployed librarian living at my parent's house with a bevy of wild animal roommates. I can see how hard that must be to resist." She rolls her eyes at me, but she's smiling. I suddenly can't not be touching her, so I reach out and brush my thumb across her flushed cheek. I watch as her breath hitches and she closes her eyes, then leans into my hand. Just a little. She's warm and soft and so, so beautiful. Like a forest sprite or an angel. My Wolf is pushing against my control to get closer to her and he gets closer to the surface than he usually does when we're not alone. She flutters her eyes open then and steps back.

"Can I get a raincheck on lunch? I ah, think I should head home now…" She whispers. I let my hand fall back down to my side and feel cold now that she's stepped away from me.

"Can I come by later?"

She presses her lips together and nods. Her eyes are fucking dazzling me as she holds my gaze while gracefully sliding into the driver's seat. I step back so she can pull her tiny car out of the lot and watch as she drives away. My Wolf growls low and I understand his frustrations completely.

"Yeah buddy, I know. We'll see her soon."

9

Ulla

I drive home on autopilot after leaving Tate at the rescue center. My head swirling with everything that happened this morning. It's hard to wrap my head around a few things. Not only had I run into Desi and Cora this morning (*Had that just been this morning??*) and felt the intense high of reconnecting with two people I love so much after so long, but I also met *him*.

Tate.

My fuckhot, intensely dreamy, this is forever, Werewolf Mate.

Hooo boy! This morning's errands definitely took an interesting detour. I give myself a little shake to clear my thoughts and take a deep breath. Or three. I'm not denying it's true. I'm not at all actually, and that's partly why it feels so strange. I should be skeptical of everything he said. But it wasn't just him. I heard his Wolf talking to me too. Well, not so much talking as sending his thoughts and feelings directly into my brain. I wasn't hearing him so much as I was knowing, and that's a new one for me.

I've heard the thoughts and feelings of animals my

whole life. As far back as I can remember, there's been a sense of what the world around me is feeling. When we lived in the city, the press of stone and steel had muffled those voices, making things a little easier. My gifts have a range to them and if I'm not surrounded by nature it's not so loud. But it also feels hollow. Like I'm only half of myself somehow. I feel better in my skin when I can touch the earth and let my spirit sink into the consciousness of the lives around me.

I pull into my parent's driveway and turn off the car. I'm not entirely sure how to explain Tate yet, so I decide to keep him to myself for now. I know I can't keep a lid on it for long, but hopefully long enough to wrap my head around things. There's another car in the drive, and I smile to myself as I grab the bag of stuff for Dennis and head inside. I can hear my mom laughing in the kitchen, her voice a little raised in animation. She's always a little louder when Aunt Alma is around. I slip my shoes off at the door and take my bag of spoils to the kitchen to say hello.

"Ah, there she is!" Alma beams at me as soon as I walk in.

Alma is the same age as Mom, but a foot taller. She looks incredible, as always. Her pale skin still smooth and the stylish French twist pulling her dark hair away from her face showcases a stunning pair of statement earrings. She stands up from her seat to wrap me up in a tight hug and then holds me out in front of her, studying me with her shrewd gaze.

"I see the time away from me has only made you more beautiful, my Darling! How do you manage it while you're surrounded by dusty old books all the time?" She pulls a leaf from my hair and tucks it into her pocket, raising an eyebrow.

"You positively glow with life today." She winks at me, and I grin at her. She'd never be content to be surrounded by quiet and books all day. Alma is a force of nature, and she needs to be in the action at all times. She often creates her own if things around her are too still.

"I'm well Auntie, thank you. And you know I love those dusty old books! They let me have grand adventures before I even have my lunch." I reply. I kiss her on her cheek and move over to kiss my mom's cheek too. Hers are a bit flushed and I glance at the bottle of wine on the counter.

"Pour yourself a glass, my Dove, and tell me absolutely everything new with you!" Alma says as she sits back into her seat with a flourish of her skirts.

"I think I'll have a cuppa instead; why don't you two finish up your conversation while I get that brewing and drop off these supplies to Dad. Is he in the garage?" I look over at my mom just as she rolls her eyes. Alma laughs and Mom snorts into her glass.

"Yes, he is. That bloody fox got into my underwear drawer somehow and they've been banished."

I bark out a surprised laugh and set out my favorite mug.

"That didn't take very long."

Alma taps her nose at Mom and the two of them burst out laughing.

"It never does Darling, babies get into everything as I recall, and foxes are generally more mischievous than most. Honestly, Katrin, you're in for an adventure this time!"

I leave the two of them to their laughter and grab the bag of fox supplies. Once I get into the mudroom, I hear my dad chatting happily and some chirping coming from the attached garage. My dad never parks the car in the garage in any of the homes we've had. He always sets it up like a man cave and it's served my parents well for both of them to have a space that's just their own. Mom took over the carriage house suite over the garage as her sewing room when they moved in here. Even though they both want their own workspaces, they still don't want to be far from each other. That makes me pause and think about Tate. What will our relationship look like in thirty years? What is our relationship right now??

With questions swirling around in my head, I open up the door to the garage and stop in my tracks. Dad's on his back in the middle of the concrete floor, while Dennis furiously attacks his left foot. The tiny kit is snarling and biting as my dad lays there and chuckles at the little ball of fluff.

"My goodness, he's a vicious little thing isn't he?" I say, closing the door behind me. There's no way I'm going to be the one to let that little maniac into the house while Mom is home. At the sound of my voice, Dennis stops his attack and scampers over to me, shaking out his dandelion fluff fur coat, wobbling on his tiny feet.

"Oh, Honey, come on up here." I croon.

I scoop him into my arms and tuck him into the crook of my neck and shoulder. He immediately settles in and licks my ear.

"You've got the magic touch, as usual, my dear," Dad says as he hauls himself up to his feet and wanders over to check out what I've brought in the bag. While he pulls out food, dishes and a soft, covered cat bed, he glances over at me.

"How pissed is your mom?"

"She's pretty mad. They're a bottle deep into the shenanigans now. Was Alma here when you got kicked out to the garage?" I ask.

"Well shit. I'll need to do something really good this time." He mutters. "Alma arrived just as your mother caught Dennis tearing through the upstairs hallway wearing her favorite bra. I honestly don't know how he got in there!" He chuckles, even while looking abashed at the situation.

"I set him down to change into inside pants and the little stinker tucked right into the closet."

"Did he get into the laundry somehow? He's too little to have opened a drawer!" I'm shaking with laughter while I imagine the scene. We've had some animal high jinx in the past, but never lingerie larceny.

"Oh hells bells." Dad grumbles and runs out of the garage and into the house. I wander slowly after him, with Dennis tucked sweetly against my shoulder. Mom and Alma are still giggling together, and I shift Dennis to tuck him into the front of my dress so I can use both hands to doctor up my tea.

"Ulla Dear, have you had a chance to pop into town since you got here?" Alma asks me sweetly. She's clearly fishing for information and I'm not sure what she's up to just yet.

"I was in town today actually. I popped into the pet store for some supplies for this little bandit and ran into Desi and Cora."

Alma claps her hands together once and then dramatically wipes imaginary sweat from her brow.

"Marvelous darling! I wasn't sure how much longer I could wait to let you girls reconnect on your own." Mom is grinning between the two of us looking pleased as well, and I just smile at the two of them. They're so lively and ridiculous.

"I've always loved that the three of you are so close." Mom sighs. "How are they both?" I look at Alma and she gestures that I should tell the tale.

"They're wonderful!" I gush. "I'd paused in the main

courtyard in town, entranced by whatever magic they were cooking up at the bakery, and Desi popped out to greet me. It's like I was never away! Their shop is more beautiful than I imagined. I can already tell that all my savings will disappear happily there." Mom laughs and reaches out to squeeze my hand on the table.

"That's why I've been avoiding it myself... I just know I'll love everything there!"

"I imagine if you saw Cora, you also got to meet her delicious fiancé?" Alma practically purrs at me.

I laugh out loud at her expression and nod.

"Yes I did. He's very tall and seems very nice. He didn't say much."

"Oh no, he doesn't at the best of times. That magnificent specimen is the epitome of the strong and silent type." Alma coos. My mom cackles at Alma's antics and the two of them dissolve into a fit of laughter.

I shake my head at them and scoop up my tea.

"I'm going to see if I can set up a safe spot for Dennis while you two finish that bottle." I kiss them both on the cheeks and go in search of my dad.

10

Tate

I clock out at General Pawspital not even an hour after Ulla left. I just can't concentrate, and Mel can see I'm not being as productive as usual.

"Get yourself out of here, Tate, Honey. Your head's not in it today."

"Sorry, Mel." I run my hands through my hair for probably the fifteenth time and I can tell it's sticking up all over the place.

"I don't know what's gotten into me." *Lies.* I'm a Liar MacLiarson. I know exactly what's gotten under my skin. A petite blonde with stormy, midnight eyes and the voice of a goddess.

"Don't you?" Mel says archly.

I look over at her and let my shoulders drop when I catch her expression.

"Is it that obvious??" I ask, grinning. I can't stop grinning. Strangers will think I'm up to something devious if I can't get myself under more control. Mel laughs at me and claps me on the shoulder as she walks past me.

"You've got the look of a man lost to a new love." She sighs then, closing her eyes for a moment.

"It's a good feeling. But unproductive as hell. Go home. Check in with your brother and see if he can find something for you to do at your *actual job*."

I chuckle as she shoos me away and I head out to my truck.

I drive home in a bit of a daze, my mind constantly running back to Ulla. What's she thinking right now? What's she doing? Is she still tingling after I touched her cheek? My hand still feels electrified and my Wolf is a smug fucker inside me.

Once home, I quickly hop into the shower to clean the sweat of the rescue center off my skin. I can't stop myself from thinking of her the whole time though; it's a miracle I don't explode the second I take myself in hand. Stroking my aching dick slowly in a tight fist, I think about her scent, the way her gorgeous brown skin blushed pink all the way down her neck, and I come so hard I see stars. Holy fuck, I'm a goner. I have to take a minute with my hand pressed against the side of the shower so I don't pass out. Again. I've never had a woman shake me up like this before and I'm fucking here for it. I clean myself up and step out of the shower to get dressed.

As I do, I see my Aunt Jett puttering around in my living room and I shriek like Mariah Carey at Christmas time. Aunt Jett spooks and jumps a good foot into the air, landing in a ready stance while holding onto what looks like my soup pot and a ladle.

"Aunt Jett," I pant, clutching my towel to my chest like a damsel in distress. "What are you doing here??"

"What?" She replies tersely. "I'm collecting the kitchenware, what does it look like I'm doing?"

"Why are you collecting *my* kitchenware, in the middle

of the afternoon? *In my apartment?*" I repeat, hoping the clarification will garner any actual clarity.

"Usain needs a special diet these days, and I'm testing recipes."

I take a deep breath and just stare at her.

Usain is her turtle. Ironically named after the famous Jamaican sprinter. A turtle that Seb and I still have no origin story for. But Jett's not a woman who feels the need to explain things to people, so we only ask the questions we really need answers to. Since I'm not planning to make soup anytime soon, these questions are not ones I need to press.

"Ok, Jett. I'm going to head into town and see if the gals need anything. Do you want me to pick up anything for you when I come back?"

"Snails and fish liver, My Boy. And a box of Fudgcicles."

I stare blankly at Jett for another moment and then shake my head. She gingerly steps through my apartment, holding the pot and ladle in one hand now and her apron, which looks suspiciously like it's full of my leftover bakery boxes, in the other.

"Bye Lovey, thanks for the pot!" She calls over her shoulder as she makes her way out. I watch her go, part of me feeling foolish for still being surprised by her unexpectedness. The other part of me making sure she gets herself all the way back into her own damned house before I lock the door and dash inside to get myself dressed. I don't want to be surprised by her again. I quickly throw on some clean clothes and run my hands through my wet hair. I don't spend much time on my appearance at the best of times. My body is in great shape due to my Wolf's need to move. I'm generally pretty active, and both my jobs allow me to maintain the muscles I've built up over the years. But

I'm not one to hit the gym. That just isn't how I want to spend my time. I'd rather head out to the woods to run with Seb or climb the ridges and mountain ranges that surround the town.

As I hop into my truck once again, I pull my phone out of my pocket and send a quick text to Desi before starting up the old engine.

TATE: **You've got some s'plaining to do.**

The little dots in the corner pop up right away as she texts me back.

DESI: **That's supposed to be my line!**

TATE: **Desi!**

DESI: **Isn't she just the best??**

TATE: **I'm on my way and I'm coming for you.**

DESI: **I already picked up more of those cookies you like.**

TATE: **All is forgiven.**

.   .   .

I'm chuckling as I pull my truck out of the drive and turn to head into town. I'm honestly not upset with Desi. I know that as much as she can see things before they come, she isn't pulling any malicious strings. Things don't happen just because she sees them. She sees things that are going to happen regardless of her visions. And I can't be mad about Ulla. I'm more interested in seeing if I can make Desi sweat. Which is pretty much impossible, since she already knows what I'm up to. So I let that shit go and hum to myself as I drive into town.

Desi's in the courtyard behind the shop when I stroll down the side alley. The girls have a pretty sweet little setup back here, with a couple of benches and lots of potted plants to keep the whole place feeling homey. I settle myself down at the picnic table in the sunshine and turn myself around so I can lean against it and look at Desi.

She's sunning herself on the bench opposite the shop's back entrance, ignoring the hell out of me. My Wolf is thrumming with excitement. He wants us to talk about Ulla, but I'm content to take this moment and appreciate my best friend. Without opening her eyes, Desi waves a hand towards the paper bag that's sitting on the table behind me. I'd smelled the cookies inside when I'd come in, but it's rude to assume. Even though I know bloody well they're for me since she teased me with them in our texts. But I still wait for her to offer them up before digging into the still warm bag.

"Have you known for long that she's my Mate?" I ask her, after swallowing the first cookie.

"Mmm hmm. I saw her coming home a few weeks ago, but not when she'd get here. Or when you'd meet. She's something else isn't she?" She asks me, peeking at me from under the lashes of one eye. Desi may be a powerful Spirit witch with gifts that are borderline terrifying, but she's a terrible actress. I smile as I roll my eyes at her attempt to be sneaky.

"She's a fucking goddess Des, and you know it. Where did she come from? How…" I trail off. I'm not even sure what I want to ask Desi now that we're sitting together. I have so many questions, but I also know that some of the answers have to come from my Mate, not my best friend.

"Ulla is the third peg in my little triad. My holy trinity of best babes. The jam in my PB & J." Desi singsongs to me. "Her family summered here the whole time we were kids but she hasn't been back in a few years. She had some growing to do."

I think back to the way Ulla's expression closed down when she mentioned her life outside of Eliza.

"Was her life away from here unpleasant?"

Desi looks at me then, her face mirroring my own concern about our girl.

"Her gifts are powerful, but she was ostracized because of them. Kids are assholes, my Precious Peach, and her heart is tender. Public school wasn't kind to her."

I growl with my Wolf at that. Never again, we vow. Now that she has us, she'll never feel the sting of a harsh word if we have anything to say about it.

Desi inhales sharply while I frown down at my fists.

"She's a little bit wounded but fiercer than she knows. *She will be tested, and her nature will be her salvation,*" Desi whispers. Her voice has gone low and flat. When I shoot my gaze sharply over to her, she's staring blankly with her head cocked to one side. Her pupils are tiny, like she's staring at the sun.

Well fuck. That's her Vision Voice.

"Hold her close but not too tight, the challenge is hers to make it right.

She'll make a choice when Moon and Mother lend her voice.

The balance shifts when the veil is thin, the shadow plots to be let in."

My heart is pounding in my chest and I can barely breathe. Desi is still locked in place and I don't dare take my eyes off her. My Wolf is dead still inside me, waiting for Desi to finish her premonition. Neither of us are willing to move for fear of losing the magic. I've never seen her have a vision like this before. Usually, she'll pause for a moment and then blink or sneeze, saying something off-hand in her light way. But this is new and terrifying.

As I watch, her whole body shudders and she slumps into the bench, her eyes rolling back into her head.

"Desi!" I shout, leaping to my feet to catch her before she slides to the ground. I catch her and hold her close to me, watching her face. She blinks up at me and frowns. Then shivers violently.

"Can I have a cookie?"

Startled by her quick topic shift, I set her gently down on the bench and snatch the bag off of the table. Handing it over to her, I scan her face. She's pale and her eyes still look a little unfocused, but otherwise she looks ok.

"Des, do you remember what you saw just now?" I ask urgently.

"You weren't supposed to hear that, Butterbear. Our girl is going to need you. But she can't know." She replies around a mouth full of almond paste and sugar.

"When Des, can you see when? Will she be in danger? Can we stop it?"

"When the sun steals the sky from the moon, the Green Man breaks the seal to force a boon." She intones, her voice shifting from her own to something deep and terrifying. Again. Oh holy hell. Then she shudders again and blinks rapidly, as if clearing something out of her eyes.

"Did Sela change the recipe on us?" She asks incredulously while she frowns at the remaining cookie in her hand. I'm too terrified to laugh at her attempt at humor.

"Oh come on, Saucy Biscuit, that was pretty funny." She nudges me. I shake myself out a little and sit back on my heels. My Wolf is thrumming with anxiety, pacing the confines of my control.

"What does that mean Des, how long do I have to save her?"

"Ah, but that's the rub, Dearest, you won't. She'll save you."

11

Ulla

D ad and I spend the rest of the afternoon setting up a little nest for Dennis in the garage. Mom is still giving them both the side eye and a wide berth, so I keep my thoughts to myself and make sure Dennis stays close to me. He's much calmer now that I'm nearby and I use my gifts to our advantage by soothing him whenever he gets too spunky.

We'll have to figure out a way to get some of his evil toddler energy out in a productive way, and I think asking Tate about it might be a good option. He's never far from my thoughts, his dreamy eyes and enticing scent popping into my mind at the slightest provocation. I've dropped what I'm doing a few times now, and Dad is looking at me with suspicion.

"Sweetie," He pauses what he's doing and sits back to look at me. "Have you got something on your mind?" He asks gently.

I look down at my hands and see that I've stacked the cans of fancy organic puppy food the clerk at the pet store recommended into a single, precarious tower.

"Uh, what makes you ask that?" I hedge.

"Well Kiddo, that's the third time you've stacked those cans in front of you instead of putting them into the cupboard where we usually keep the rescue food. I just thought, maybe something is distracting you." He smiles as he says it and I blush when I realize he's right. I've been re-stacking my little tower over and over again in a daze. A Tate daze. A Mate Tate daze. I giggle a little hysterically and cover my face with my hands.

"Oh boy. I've seen that look before." Dad groans.

"What?? You have?" I ask, in embarrassed astonishment. I don't remember being gonzo over a boy before. Certainly not around my dad. Oh hells, this is embarrassing!

"You were fifteen I think, and you had those posters of that band on your door, who was it... Going Somewhere? Looking for Directions?? Crikey Kiddo, I don't remember what they were called, but there was a lot of hair flipping and you were obsessed with them. Don't you remember?"

"Ohmygoooods Dad! *One Direction*??"

"That sounds familiar. So much hair gel." He chuckles to himself and I throw my head back and laugh. Dennis startles inside the little, cozy cat tent he's dozing in. My embarrassment eases out of me and I apologize to Dennis for interrupting his nap.

"Yeah Dad, I may have had a crush on one of those boys. In my defense, they were a bit of a phenomenon."

"Oh don't try that with me. You used to write your name over and over again with different last names depending on which of those boys' faces you could see the least!"

"Dad! That's not true! I only had eyes for Harry. And he has beautiful hair."

"*Has*?! You still follow that garbage?" My dad is

howling with laughter now and I can't help but join in. It feels so good to be silly with him again, just like when I was little. The door to the garage opens up then, Alma and Mom coming in to investigate.

"What on earth has gotten into you two out here?" Mom asks us. It only makes Dad and I laugh harder. Mom rolls her eyes, but I catch Alma watching me with a gleam in her eye. As I catch my breath and wipe the tears from my cheeks, I bump my shoulder into my dad's and help him put away the last of the food cans I've been too distracted to deal with properly so far.

"Ulla my Darling," Aunt Alma purrs. "Whatever did you get up to today?"

I press my lips together to hide my smile, but I can't stop the flush from rushing over my cheeks.

"Oh this is gorgeous, do tell!" Alma wiggles her eyebrows suggestively and I laugh again. I walk towards the door to get back into the house, kissing her cheek as I move past her.

"I may have met someone interesting today, Auntie," I say coyly.

"Katrin!" Alma crows, clapping her hands together and startling poor Dennis again. "Uncork that red, I'm staying until I hear absolutely everything! Should we order in?"

Ten minutes later we're all sitting together at the kitchen table, laughing and enjoying being together. I haven't said anything about Tate yet, but we've talked about Desi and Cora and my decision to visit the Rescue Center. Mom has increased in volume by a few decibels and Dad has now joined in, although he never drinks more than one glass. Alma is still imbibing, but her gaze is clear and sharp and I have the feeling that some of her exuberance is not wine related anymore. Her focus is too shrewd, she's waiting for me to spill the beans and I'm hesitant to share too much.

So I keep the werewolf information to myself and just stick to the nitty gritty.

"Alright Kiddo, you've kept us on pins and needles for long enough. Tell us what has you blushing so adorably!" Mom says. Dad just raises his eyebrows and Alma takes a sip from her glass. I clear my throat and take a deep breath. My parents are open minded and wonderful people, but I'm still their little girl. We don't have a ton of history talking about the boys in my life. Although Tate is no boy… oh Gods, I'm blushing even more!

As I begin telling them about my trip to the rescue center and how I met Tate, Dad breaks in with, "He's a great guy, I've chatted with him a few times over the last year, and he really knows his stuff. Great with animals." I feel my cheeks heat and glance at Alma, who grins like the Cheshire Cat. Taking a deep breath and a sip of my tea, I continue telling them an abbreviated version of the after-noon's events.

Both of my parents are watching me with twinkling eyes as I finish my story. They look at each other and smile warmly. They're still so sweet together after all this time and I smile back at them. I glance over at Alma and see that she's watching me too. Her expression is a little smug somehow.

"Did you get his number?" She asks me.

"Oh, no, I didn't think to ask for it!" It feels like the wind in my sails has suddenly dropped and my shoulders slump. I blink a few times and realize I'm really disap-pointed in myself for not thinking of that sooner. He'd asked if he could come by later, but he doesn't know where I live! I'm not sure how long I want to wait before I see him again. I wish he was here now frankly. That's a little silly though isn't it? I saw him just a couple of hours ago.

Alma's lips curl up on one side and I can't figure out why she's looking at me like that, when Dennis suddenly perks up and starts chirping. He's been curled up in my Dad's lap while we've been chatting at the table, but he scrabbles down and is snarling in his adorable baby way.

I look down at him, feeling his disquiet, but not able to suss out why. His thoughts are a jumble of instincts so I can't pinpoint what set him off. A knock at the door has all of us swinging our heads to look towards the front of the house and Dennis starts growling. Alma is grinning.

12

Tate

I carry Desi into the shop and call in the cavalry. Once I get some more cookies into her and fetch her a cup of tea, she settles more into herself. That's quite possibly the most terrifying thing I've ever seen. Cora had exclaimed and fussed over Des when I brought her inside, noticing right away how pale she was and how she shook. I imagine I don't look any better. Seb is here too, he's never far from Cora anymore, and he frowns at me as he glares in my direction.

"What the hell man, what happened?" He asks in his gruff way.

"She had a vision of my Mate, and it's bad."

"Wait, did you just say your *Mate?*" He puts his hand on my shoulder and pulls me to look at him. He searches my eyes with a frown and I take a deep breath.

"Shit, yes I did. Fuck. Brother, it's been a day and a half." I run my hand through my hair and try to calm my racing thoughts. Has it really only been since this morning that my whole world shifted under me? How is it possible

I'm so caught up in Ulla when we've only just met? How can I feel this way already? My Wolf is pacing, snarling inside me and I can feel him tearing at the edges of my control. Seb's Wolf sends a thread of calm through the pack bonds to me, and I feel my own Wolf gratefully settle a little bit.

"Talk to me man," My brother says. His voice is gentle, his eyes full of understanding.

"How did you do it for so long?" I blurt out.

"Do what?"

"Hold your Wolf in check. Once you'd scented Cora that day at the market, it was nearly a year before she accepted the bond. How did you not lose your fucking mind?"

He huffs out a breath and looks at me ruefully.

"You saw me, I was a mess. But I couldn't scare her off. Or at least I tried not to. I didn't know how to approach her and was so worried about spooking her that I was an asshole. To everyone." He looks embarrassed as he rubs the back of his neck.

"My Wolf wasn't pleased with me, but he was able to keep an eye on her and that helped." He adds.

I think about how Ulla and I met. How she spoke to my Wolf and wasn't spooked at all. Or at least not enough to run. She seemed more intrigued and embarrassed than anything. But I think about how I could also scent her arousal, and my Wolf's pacing turns to purring as we focus on that.

"When I met her this morning, she wasn't spooked. She was shockingly
accepting of the whole thing," I say softly.

"You met her this morning?!" Seb barks. "Where? Who is she?"

I can hear Cora on the other side of the room still

fussing over Desi. I turn to look at them and nod my head toward them.

"Let's sit with the girls, I have a feeling Desi has more to add, and Cora will want to hear this too."

We make our way over to them and I crouch on the floor in front of Desi. Cora wrings her hands as she steps back and Seb envelopes his bigger body around her.

"What's going on, Tate?" Cora demands. Her voice is low, and I notice the hair around her face is floating gently. Not a sign that she's feeling calm and in control. She often has it pulled up or braided so it doesn't give away her feelings when she's agitated. But I remember how it whipped around her like a vortex not that long ago, when her Mate Bond had scared the shit out of her and she fought against it. Now that I know it's one of her tells, I keep an eye on it to gauge her moods. Taking a deep breath I look at Desi and she nods.

"I met my Mate this morning."

"Your Mate?!" Cora practically shrieks. "That's amazing! But what does that have to do with Desi and why she looks like she's been on a three day bender?"

Desi chuffs a laugh and waves a dismissive hand towards Cora.

"Flatterer," She says softly. Cora rolls her eyes and then sets her gaze on me.

"Spill it, Tate, what's going on?"

"You know her." I start. "Ulla is my Mate."

"What in the ever-loving fuck??" Cora practically shouts, but her expression is mostly joy. Then a quick shift to confusion as she blinks between Desi and I.

"Wait. Hold up. When the fuck did you meet Ulla and what did you see that has you both looking like you've seen a ghost??"

Desi chuckles then and slowly stands up.

"Relax, Mama Bear. No ghosts were seen. But something's coming and Ulla's at the heart of it all," Desi says softly.

Cora moves to Desi's side and tries to help her. Desi just swats her hands away and leans over to kiss Cora's cheek.

"We've got some time before things get weird. Let the man enjoy being Mated before we throw loose peanut butter all over things."

We all look at Desi then.

"It's messy and greasy and hard to clean up. Jeez you guys, tough crowd." She mutters as she grabs another cookie from the bag I'd set on the counter.

"Tell me everything!" Cora demands and I smile to see the excitement in her eyes. I settle my hip against the counter and cross my arms over my chest. I tell them about Ulla coming into the rescue center and how she calmed Daisy so effortlessly. I tell them about how she spoke directly to my Wolf and how not freaked out at all she seems, which is still baffling to me.

"Wait," Cora interrupts. "What do you mean she spoke directly to your Wolf? How did she know?"

"That's the thing! I didn't tell her, she just knew and rolled with it and they have a whole connection already where he just talks to her. I've never heard of something like this happening before."

Seb grunts next to Cora and frowns in thought.

"What is that? What's that grunt all about?" Cora asks as she looks up at him.

"I'm just thinking about when I met her this morning. Her energy is …interesting."

Desi snorts into her teacup and we all glance over at her. Cora's eyes flash.

"What do you know, Desiree Soliel Gibson??"

Oh shit. People don't pull out full names unless shit is about to get real.

Rolling her eyes, Desi holds her cup in her hands and tilts her head to the side.

"Ulla has always had a connection to animals, Pumpkin Pie, you know this. It's not so surprising that she can hear Tate's Wolf. The way you two grumble and growl isn't exactly subtle."

"I'm not buying it, you know something."

"Maybe I do, maybe I don't. All will become clear in time."

Cora throws her hands up in the air and huffs in exasperation. "UGH! Desi, I love you, but I hate it when you get all Mysterious Wise Woman on me. Throw me a bone here!"

Desi laughs and gets up to refresh her tea.

"It's not my bone to throw." She says.

Cora stomps her foot and mutters an adorable string of profanities. Seb smiles down at her and lets her fume. I look over at Desi and catch her watching me.

"I think you should court her, my All Beef Patty." She says firmly. I laugh, shaking my head. She beams at me and I realize she stepped up her nickname game to redirect our mood. But she's right in this. I want to court her too. Ulla asked me if I was her werewolf boyfriend, and honestly, that sounds like a good place to start. My Wolf needs her like I need air. My resolve strengthens the more I think about it. Maybe something scary is coming. But worrying over it isn't going to solve the problem tonight and all I want is to have Ulla in my arms. That's something I can deal with right now.

"I've got to go." I say to the room at large.

"Take those flowers from the pottery display and swing by the bakery for a chocolate croissant." Desi suggests. Her smile is bright and it feels like the heavy fog from her vision earlier is lifting. I won't let my guard down for a second, but I'll woo my Mate while I keep her close to me.

13

Ulla

I look at Alma's shit-eating grin and suspect I know who's on the other side of that door. My heart pounds in my chest and butterflies go bananas in my belly. But he doesn't know where I live; we hadn't exchanged numbers or anything earlier.

"Are you going to get the door, Ulla dear, or just stare at it like a deer in the headlights?" Mom asks me. I blink and give myself a little shake.

"Yeah, I'll get it," I say softly. I smooth my hands down my skirt and frown at Dennis; the little kit is still growling. I can't see who's on the other side, but there's a pull in my chest that feels like a confirmation of my suspicions. Like there's an invisible rope pulling me towards whoever it is. Or like lights are being flicked on in an empty house. I'm being pulled home.

Tate is still as gorgeous as he was this morning when I slowly pull the door open. He holds a bundle of flowers and a paper bag that smells heavenly. His expression is fierce, intense even. Not an angry face, but he looks serious as he gazes down at me.

"Hey."

"Hey." He inhales deeply and closes his eyes, his whole body trembling for a moment, like he's resetting himself somehow. His Wolf looks out at me when he slowly opens his eyes again and I smile.

"Hey to you too."

Tate chuckles softly then and hits me with a real smile, and I have to grip the doorframe tightly in my hands so I don't faint dead at his feet. It's so unfair how beautiful he is. He's changed his clothes since I last saw him. No longer in faded, ripped jeans and a t-shirt so old it could have grandbaby shirts. Oh no. He's wearing considerably nicer dark jeans and a crisp white t-shirt that leaves zero doubts about how hard and big his chest is. He's washed his hair too and it's shiny and tousled in a way some people spend a lot of time on, but I can tell that his is just like that with no effort. I bet he just wakes up every day looking like good sex come to life. I bring my hand up to my chin to make sure I'm not drooling. I hear his Wolf chuckle at that and Tate's mouth quirks up in a grin.

A chair squeaks behind me, and I remember in a rush of mortification that my parents and Alma are right behind me, watching my personal wet dreams unfold at the front door. My cheeks flush hot and I drop my face into my hands, groaning my embarrassment.

"Well now, Ulla dear, do invite your friend inside to say hello." Alma practically purrs from the kitchen. Tate glances over my shoulder quickly and smiles wider when he sees the peanut gallery.

"Evening, Alma. It's a pleasure to see you, as always," Tate says easily, his voice so deep and smooth that I have to blink myself out of my stupor. Oh wow. He's good. I clear my throat and step away from the door frame.

"Uh, would you like to come inside and subject yourself to parental scrutiny? I warn you, the ladies are at least a bottle deep and I expect them to be wildly inappropriate."

He presses his lips together to contain his grin, all lopsided and adorable, and I swear my panties start singing. His eyes darken and he takes a slow step towards me. I hold my ground, looking up into his smoldering gaze, and godsdamnit I'm panting! All he did was step towards me looking like all my fantasies come to life and I'm ready to throw him down on the ground and ride him like a carnival carousel horse. On my parent's front porch. His Wolf sends me a flash of his own inspiration and I nearly pass out.

"Gnnnh" I whisper.

Tate leans down towards me and rubs his cheek along mine, slow enough that I can feel the soft warmth of his cheek whisper against mine. It's the sweetest, softest touch and I'm utterly done for. He inhales deeply as he caresses his nose into my hair and I'm suddenly so wet and hot all over that I whimper into his neck.

"I want to court you properly, Ulla Mine…" He says softly into my ear, his breath tickling my overheated skin and sending a lick of heat flaring down to my toes. His Wolf growls low in agreement and having them both seducing me at the same time makes me feel like a powerful sex Goddess and I'm not sure I can say no even if I want to. And I definitely don't want to say no. I'm saying all of the yesses. Tate is pumping out some serious pheromones that even Venus herself wouldn't be able to resist. I tremble and nod. My voice is lost somewhere with my senses and I put my free hand on his chest.

Oh wow. Systems overload! He's so hot, physical heat radiates from him and he's rumbling deep in his chest. I look sharply up into his face as I realize his heart is beating just as fast as mine.

"I want to be your werewolf boyfriend." His gaze is open and yearning and I want to kiss him so badly. His rumbling turns into a purr, his wolfish smile telling me, as much as the Wolf inside of him is, just how much of that thought he heard. I clear my throat again and try to use my words.

"Yes please." Is all my addled brain will allow.

He chuckles against my heated cheek and then he presses a tender kiss against my furious blush. Fireworks explode in my stomach and I huff out a deep breath. He straightens then, and looks past me to my family. I shake myself to reset my flummoxed senses and slowly turn to look at them too.

Both of my parents are staring at us. My mother is slightly slack-jawed and Dad looks a little thrown. But Alma... Alma looks like the cat that ate the canary. Her smug expression roams over both Tate and I, and she leans back in her chair.

"Well isn't this a delightful turn of events?" She says, steepling her fingers like Dr. Evil, and I snort despite my fluttering heart.

"You O'Connell boys certainly know how to make an entrance."

14

Tate

Tracking Ulla to her parent's house isn't hard. Her scent is locked into my mind and letting my Wolf close to the surface allows us to catch it quickly. Once I leave the gang at the girl's shop and make a quick stop at Butter My Muffin, I make it to Ulla's parent's place in short order. They live in a decently big, Cape Cod style house, close to the edge of a copse of spruce trees and my Wolf rumbles his approval. He likes that we can run all the way to her house if we want to. I want to tuck her into my side and never leave her. I'm still surprised at how drawn to her I feel. How just the thought of her calms my Wolf and sets my blood to singing. I feel like I've woken up from living a half-dream life to discover the real world is full of brightness and music. I'm a fucking Hallmark card and I'm not mad about it. I've always been a pretty upbeat guy. Not like Seb and his near-constant grumbling. While I try to always find the bright side of things, my Wolf still yearns for more Pack. I've come to realize I need the press of energy, the knowledge that we have a place in a more structured family. Cora and Desi becoming part of our family Pack has made some of this settle for me, but now that I know Ulla exists, that I'm hers, I feel like I'm on top of the world and can't stop smiling.

Thinking about Desi's premonition dulls my joy, but she's adamant that we have time to prepare for whatever is coming, and I'm determined to head it off before whatever it is gets here. I'm not going to let anything happen to Ulla now that I've found her. No matter what Desi saw coming, I'll protect Ulla, with my life if I have to. My Wolf growls in agreement, pacing the confines of my control with his fierce intent. Whatever is coming, we have this time now with our Mate, and we both intend to make the most of it.

When I step onto the front porch, I hear laughing inside. Judging by the scents swirling around me, I can tell that Ulla's home, and her parents are inside with her. I sniff out that Cora's mother is here too. We have a teasing relationship that we both enjoy. Mostly to drive my brother bonkers, which we both also make the most of. The grumpy asshole makes it a little too easy sometimes, but Alma and I never miss an opportunity to rile him up. I take a moment to appreciate how tightly woven this small town is. That Alma is practically my mother-in-law through Seb, and also a part of my Mate's life, feels like another piece of this strange mystical puzzle linking us together. I've never been overly superstitious, but this is a coincidence too big to ignore.

I can hear Ulla's soft voice inside and the rumble of the other voices. My Wolf's ears prick up when I hear her say it was nice to chat with a cute guy. I stand a little taller as I realize she's telling her family about meeting me.

Who else could she have met today besides her Fated Mate, that she'd be talking about? I preen a little, knowing that she thinks I'm cute. I don't spend a lot of time primping or thinking about my appearance, but I *am* a werewolf. Our magical genetics are a bit of a social advantage. We're generally bigger and more muscular than our human competition, and I've had my fair share of looks from the ladies I've run into in the past. I'm not ashamed to admit that I'm a flirt, and I've used my handsome mug to charm my way into a few beds over the last few years. Since we moved here to Eliza Falls though, I haven't hooked up with anyone but Desi. After we both realized pretty quickly that we aren't meant to be together biblically, I've been happy to just be on my own.

I step up to the door and knock. The conversation inside stops and I listen to what I assume is Dennis the fox kit growling. Ulla hadn't mentioned that they had any other animals in the house besides the fox and the snake. I hear Alma softly say something and then light footsteps heading towards me. My heart thunders in my chest, just knowing that she's coming towards me. I allow my Wolf to inhale her scent and let it swirl around in my mind, settling into all of my empty spaces. The door slowly swings open and there she is. My luscious Mate is looking up at me with a look of wonder in her eyes. I feel a swift surge of adrenaline scream through my body and the pull towards her increases. She's so fucking lovely. She's still wearing the same dress as earlier today, and her dainty feet are bare. I notice her toes curl into the carpet and her hand is tight on the doorframe. I can't resist the pull of her and I push down into her space, breathing in her scent and allowing myself, and my Wolf, to mark her softly with our own. The press of her cheek against mine sends my brain spiraling into the universe like a comet and it takes all of my strength to pull myself back and not devour her right here on the front porch. Her breath hitches like a siren song and only the rustle of the other people in the room pulls me out of my daze. It's shockingly easy to get lost in her nearness. I clear my throat and straighten as I acknowledge her family watching us, Alma openly grinning while Ulla's parents look a little shell-shocked by my overt display of affection.

"I'm sorry to just pop in like this, but I was too excited to see Ulla again."

I watch Ulla's mom close her jaw sharply and her dad chuckle at her when he hears her teeth click together.

"Well that's certainly a nice thing to hear, isn't it Katrin?" He says, "A nice young man taking the initiative to come calling on our daughter."

He's still watching Katrin's reactions as she visibly pulls herself together. She's an elegant black woman with light brown skin, wearing a set of matching silk pajamas in deep green.

"Good grief they're making men quite attractive these days." She mutters to herself. I hold in my chuckle so I don't make her uncomfortable. I don't know how much they know about me, but I'm guessing Ulla didn't tell them I'm a werewolf and have extra keen senses. That's something we can save for a special occasion. I look at Alma, she's still sitting at the kitchen table as if she's actually sitting in a throne room and I wink at her. She knows what Seb and I are. Cora would've been hard pressed to keep that a secret from her mother for long. Alma is a very perceptive woman and her gifts as an Artifact witch give her a leg up in any investigating she chooses to do. As it is, our supernatural nature is something that binds us together. I wonder how much Ulla's family knows and what their gifts are. I get a distinctly human vibe from them both, which is surprising considering how powerful their daughter is but I remember that Alma and Katrin are old friends. It doesn't matter where she came from, she's mine and I plan to treasure her.

Ulla shakes herself again and blinks up at me. She takes a deep, centering breath and then slips her hand into mine. Her small fingers are warm, and I feel that small touch slide over my skin like cool water on a hot day. I sense her nervousness but it's overridden by a wave of calm that settles over my shoulders like a blanket. I take a moment to wonder if this is part of her gift, if this peace that's settled over me is what Daisy felt at the rescue center earlier. I wonder if Ulla knows she's doing it or if it's something that just emanates from her. I'll ask her soon, but not tonight. Tonight I just want to soak up her nearness and spend as much time as I can being close to her.

I squeeze her hand and smile down at her. She's so petite that she can tuck in easily under my arm. The thought makes me smile wider and her answering grin lights up her whole face.

"Did you hear that thought?" I ask her.

Her eyes twinkle and she bites the corner of her bottom lip again and I'm transfixed. Jesus and all the dryads, she's beautiful. My Wolf purrs his agreement and she blushes a little more.

"Get in here you two," Abe cajoles. Ulla blinks and grins ruefully, ducking her head. Alma's laughter chimes through the room and she claps her hands, making her bracelets jangle.

"Tate dear, are you hungry? We've got a mountain of take-out tonight, I was left in charge of ordering dinner and I may have gone a little overboard after a glass too many."

15

Ulla

Tate sits next to me, squeezed in at my parent's old kitchen table and it feels… wonderful. It feels *right*, that he's tucked into the dining nook and charming everyone around him. He's so easy to talk to. Both of my parents are happily chatting away, none of the awkwardness I expected when I imagined introducing them to a man in my life. This has never really happened before. I'd been such a loner throughout school, before switching to a distance education model, that I didn't bring friends home at all. Cora and Desi were the exceptions. The few men I'd briefly dated back in Vancouver were never invited home to meet my family. But watching Tate fit himself right into my life so easily felt good. I'm getting waves of contentment from his Wolf, particularly when we're touching in some way. A brush of our shoulders or the press of our knees under the table. I try not to jump and blush everytime my skin grazes against Tate's, but it's a losing battle. Alma's watching me like a hawk and I can't quite interpret her smirk. Although I've known her long enough to assume she's likely enjoying watching me squirm, I know she enjoys all the drama. Me bringing a man home to my parents for the first time is probably catnip for her. But as I think about it, I realize that I don't mind her interest. Alma is a whirlwind, much like Cora, but there's nothing but love between us. So I straighten my shoulders and lean into Tate a bit more. Something I've wanted to do since he sat down next to me. His Wolf rumbling in his chest tells me he's pleased with the connection too.

I look up at him then and take in the line of his jaw, the way his tousled hair curls a little at the nape of his neck and over his ear. I trace the edge of his nose with my gaze, and watch the laugh lines around his eyes crease as he laughs at something my dad says. I'm barely paying any attention to the conversation. I'm entirely caught up in the man next to me. He charmed Dennis shortly after he arrived, the little ball of fluff currently tucked into a sleepy ball on his lap. It had only taken him a moment of eye contact with the kit before Dennis flopped onto his back and was madly in love with him. I felt his Wolf send waves of calm over the little fox and Dennis is now putty in his hands. Everything about Tate feels magical and delicious. I'm smitten and pretty ok with it.

Oh who am I kidding? I'm fangirling hard.

Sighing at the inevitability, accepting that this is exactly where I want to be, I tuck myself even closer to Tate's warm body and bliss out a little when he pulls his heavy arm around me. He looks down at me smiling, his hazel eyes twinkling. His Wolf sends a pleased growly purr down his chest and I grin at his smug satisfaction. He's pleased that I'm claiming them in this small way in front of my family.

"Oh good gracious, this is delightful!" Mom squeals. I think she's been waiting for me to bring a date home for a while. She's a staunch feminist, but also a hopeless romantic. A dynamic that often pulls against itself. But I know that ultimately she wants me to be happy with a partner who supports me, whoever they may be. I haven't given her many opportunities to see me with anyone, and it seems like she's soaking up all the satisfied maternal feelings she can.

We stay like this for what feels like hours and also a blink of an eye, Tate holding me against his side while we chat easily with my family. Mom and Alma finish off another bottle of wine together and shortly afterwards my dad makes an executive decision.

"Alright ladies, it's time to wrap this up! Both of you are going to chug a big glass of water and I'm going to pop some waffles into the toaster. Ulla Honey, please settle Dennis into his little den. Tate, it's a pleasure to meet you, but I need to take care of my gals." Dad stands up and reaches his hand across the table to Tate, who passes a sleeping Dennis over to me before uncurling himself from my side to shake it. A moment of primal fatherly communication passes between them. As if they're speaking mind to mind, Tate nods and Dad nods back and then the spell is broken and I roll my eyes at both of them.

"Come on little flurff, let's get you settled in for the night," I say into the kit's cloud of fur. He smells so good, warm and a little spicy. He stretches and yawns as I walk slowly to the garage, but stays sleeping as I gently place him into the soft cat cave we've set up for him. I wrap the towel around the front of the entrance to keep the heat inside for him and then close the kennel door. We have his soft nest tucked into the bigger kennel to keep Dennis contained while we aren't with him and hopefully he'll stay comfortable all night. Although I expect my dad to pull him out of there at the first yip when Dennis wakes up. I send him a wave of sleepy thoughts to help him get a few more hours, check to make sure the baby monitor Dad has out here for Dennis is plugged in, and then turn to go back into the kitchen.

Tate is standing in the doorway, watching me with glittering eyes. He's leaning against one side of the frame with his arms crossed over his chest. The way his arms fill out the sleeves of his t-shirt and the snug stretch of the fabric across his broad shoulders makes my breath hitch in my throat. I imagine him running his hands through his hair and watching the hem of his shirt riding up to expose his abs. I bet they're lean and hard and oh Gods, I'm totally perving on him to his face. I feel my cheeks flush and watch as his eyes grow darker and hear his breathing change.

"I can smell your heat, Ulla Mine, I like what you're telling my Wolf."

An embarrassed giggle that sounds more like a whimper escapes me and I cover my flaming cheeks with my hands. Tate slowly pushes himself from the doorframe and stalks toward me. So slowly, like he doesn't want to spook me. I straighten my spine and force my hands away from my face. I grab fistfuls of my skirt and watch him prowl over to me, his hungry gaze melting my underwear. My whole body feels flushed with heat and I can't take my eyes away from him. He's just so *alive*.

My breathing is sharp and uneven like I've been running, and I can feel the skin between my shoulder blades grow tight as I hold myself utterly still. Not out of fear, I feel completely safe with Tate, but in anticipation. I want to kiss him, feel his rough stubble against my cheek again. The Wolf is rumbling steadily now, I can hear him from where I stand. Tate's only a few feet from me and the heat from his body feels like a third person in the room. Everything about him is vital. He's standing in front of me, looking down at me with hunger and awe in his eyes.

"Finding your Mate is rare, did you know that?" He asks me in his growly, low voice. I can feel his breath against my skin and goosebumps flare up all down my arms and back. I shake my head while I stare into his eyes. I don't know if I could speak if I tried. My throat feels tight, and my breath is nearly heaving. The front of my dress feels tight against my breasts, like the fabric can barely contain my flesh, and I'm close to swooning.

His hands reach out and he gently, so gently, strokes my upper arms up towards my shoulders. I'm rooted to the spot, taught like a bowstring.

"Breathe, Ulla, I've got you." He whispers. I blink quickly and shudder a breath through my body, stumbling a little closer towards him. I flex my hands and release the death grip I have on my dress and lift my hands up to touch his hips. His eyes close and he groans as I feel the heat of his skin through his t-shirt.

16

Tate

I feel her small hands move up to touch my sides and I groan low when the heat of her fingers touches me through the material of my shirt. I feel branded. Like she's put her mark on me for everyone to see. It's absurd, it's just the lightest touch. But because it's her, *my Mate*, it feels like a benediction.

I smooth my hands up her arms and over her shoulders to cup her slender neck. I'm in awe of her. She's the most amazing creature I've ever seen and I feel the pull of the bond snapping between us as I continue to stare into her dark eyes. I've never seen eyes like hers before, their color a blue so dark they're almost black, but swimming with flecks of gold like stars. Right now her pupils are so big that the midnight is almost entirely swallowed by her desire.

My fingers twitch as I run my thumbs along the edge of her jaw and her lips part on a ragged inhale.

"Tate," She whispers. My name on her lips sends a jolt of pleasure through my whole body, all the way down to my toes. I bring my face closer to hers, to be able to breathe her warm breath directly into my lungs. I feel her hands grip the fabric of my shirt like she can't help but hold me tighter, and my Wolf pushes close to the surface of my control. I feel him looking down at her through my eyes and she doesn't flinch. She fucking smiles at him, her acceptance of the beast inside of me throwing me over the edge of the cliff I've been grasping for dear life.

"Tate, please." Her voice is barely a dream against my skin, so soft that I could be imagining it. She licks her lower lip and my Wolf snarls his pleasure through me. She presses closer and I stroke my nose along her cheek and jaw, breathing in her scent like I can hold it inside my body. She's trembling and I tenderly glide my hands farther into her soft hair. My palms skate over her ears and she tilts her face up, a supplication. I can't deny her anything. I move my mouth over her skin, feeling the softness of her under my lips until I feel her breath against my own. I press my mouth against hers in the lightest kiss I can manage. My Wolf is teetering on the edge of madness, his pleasure so keen and bright, it feels like a knife in my heart. Her hands slide up my back, roaming up my spine to my shoulders, and she pushes her mouth closer to mine. Her lips are so soft, so warm and her breath is sweet against mine. It feels like our souls are blending together in this kiss and I'm only too happy to tumble into her. She presses the length of her body against mine, sliding her hands tighter around my ribs, her tongue teasing the seam of my mouth.

I'm *lost*. Like a wave crashing over me, the sensation of her warm, wet tongue sliding into my mouth sends me swirling into a sea of desire and desperation I've never encountered before. I groan again as I deepen the kiss, sweeping my tongue against hers and claiming her in this moment. My hands are still in her hair, pulling at the cloud-like strands of it, and I nip at her bottom lip. She shudders, a delicate whimper escaping her and I breathe it in, deep into my soul. I can't let any part of her escape me and I take her soft moans into myself. I trail my mouth along her jaw, using my lips and teeth along her skin and she clasps her arms around me tighter. Inhaling her scent as I move my mouth to her ear, I can barely control the Wolf inside me. He's desperate to fully claim her, make her ours. Her hands have made their way into my hair now and I love how she fists it so tightly, like she isn't even aware of how desperate she is. I am. Her heady scent is swirling around me and I'm helpless. I want to worship at her feet and offer everything I am at the altar of her body.

I tighten my arms around her and pull her against me. She responds by wrapping her legs around my hips and the heat, oh Gods, the heat between her legs pressing against my rigid, straining cock is going to kill me. I've never been so hard in my life. I adjust my hold on her body to hold her up, my hands gripping her ass and she moans deeper into my mouth.

I growl and kiss her harder. Our teeth click together, our breathing is ragged, we're becoming untamed and we're heading to the point of no return. Struggling for control, I try to reign in my need for her and think. But she's rocking her hips against me now and I'm seeing stars. *Oh fuck*, she feels so good. I pull my mouth away from hers, kissing along her neck again and try to breathe around the desperation my Wolf is howling through me.

The need to claim her completely is becoming over-whelming, but we're in her parent's garage. Making out like teenagers sneaking around past curfew. A rustling behind us wakes me up out of the haze of lust I'm swirling in and I slow us down. I soften the kiss and blink myself back to reality. We're both breathing hard and Ulla blinks her eyes open to stare into mine.

"Whuh," She whispers. The confusion in her gaze is

adorable and I rub the tip of my nose against hers. She hears the rustling then too and looks over my shoulder, when she locks her eyes onto the source of the sound she grins.

"How did you get out here?" She asks softly, her voice is raspy velvet, rough from the need still pumping between us. I turn us to look at what has her attention and twitch when I come face to face with shiny black eyes and delicate scales.

"Suzanne, I presume?" I chuckle. The snake is surprisingly beautiful, her scales a mottled tan and brown with black spots all over her body. She's not as big as I expected her to be, but still big enough that I instinctively hold Ulla tighter. Ulla huffs a quiet laugh and wiggles in an attempt to get down. I growl as I reluctantly release her until her bare feet touch the floor. The sensation of her body sliding down over my erection forces my eyes closed and I fist my hands in the fabric of her dress as I shudder some sense back into my addled brain.

I would have claimed her here in her parent's garage if Suzanne hadn't distracted us. As much as I need to sink into her and claim her as my Wolf is so desperate to, I want to be able to take my time and savor every moment. I want to swallow all of her moans and drive her over the edge with every touch. I can't do that here, where her parents could hear her. I shake my head and let go of her dress. Ulla bites her bottom lip and shoots me a half grin full of understanding and reluctant acceptance.

"I really like kissing you." She says in a conspiratorial whisper.

I bark out a laugh and run a hand through my hair. It's all over the place from her hands tugging at it, and I smile to think that she feels as desperate as I do.

"I've never been cock blocked by a snake before" I grin

down at her. That's something I never thought I'd ever say. Her delicate snort makes me grin even wider, and I look over to where Suzanne is coiled patiently on the top of the standing freezer behind us. Ulla clears her throat and looks up at me again from under her lashes, her expression suddenly shy.

"I'm going to take her inside, it's not warm enough for her to stay out here for too long."

I step back so she can comfortably scoop Suzanne off the top of the freezer and wait for her to get the big snake settled in her arms. Suzanne softly nudges Ulla and works her way over her shoulders and I can tell they're sending sweet thoughts to each other. Ulla's expression is a little distant, a soft smile on her kiss-swollen lips. She blinks before looking back up at me and her soft smile transforms into something deep and shining, her eyes creasing at the corners and her nose wrinkling.

"Well sir, perhaps we should take this as a sign and call it a night. I'd love to see you again, hopefully soon?" Her voice lifts at the end with hope in her eyes and I shove my hands into my pockets, smiling right back at her.

"Are you free tomorrow?"

17

Ulla

I take my time getting Suzanne tucked into her big terrarium in the living room. Once she's settled, I quietly make my way upstairs to my bedroom. I have to pass Alma snoring in the guest bedroom to get to it and I press my lips together to stifle my giddy laughter. I barely contain myself until I get into my room, throw myself onto my bed and scream into my pillow.

Oh holy sex bomb Batman, Tate can really kiss. Like every romance novel's first kiss scene rolled into one talented tongue. My whole body is positively thrumming and I kick my legs and thrash my body all over my bed to get some of the energy out. Like a kid on Christmas morning, I can barely contain myself and I love every minute of it. I don't think I've ever felt like this about a boy before. Oh Gods who am I kidding? Tate is a big hulking *man* and I can't wait for tomorrow. I heave deep breaths and attempt to calm my body down enough to sleep. It feels like a useless endeavor when all I can think about are his eyes and the way he looked like he wanted to devour me whole. How his hands are rough and calloused, but he touches me so sweetly. I let my mind run through our kiss in the garage, and heat shudders through my whole body. I can feel how slick I am between my thighs and I regret that we didn't explore this new magic between us a little farther. I mean, one orgasm would've been alright with me. In fact, I'll probably fall asleep much faster if I take matters into my own hands, just real quick and quiet. I scramble out of my dress and under the covers. There's a little voice in the very back of my mind reminding me that my parents and my aunt are only a few walls away from me and that takes some of the romance out of the air. But the silky sheets sliding over my legs and the way my tight nipples feel as I squirm a little are louder. My body is desperate for a release and thoughts of Tate's soft lips and his sexy as hell growls, oh Gods, he actually *growls at me* when he's kissing me! Those thoughts win out and I slowly glide my hand down to cup my pussy. I'm so wet and I know the ache won't be satisfied with just a swirl of my fingers over my clit. I need to feel full, so I slip two fingers inside and feel my walls clench around my own fingers. It doesn't take long to bring myself to climax, Tate's name on my lips as I gasp my satisfaction. Sleep pulls me under soon after and I dream about a golden Wolf running towards me with hungry eyes.

I wake up tangled in my sheets and drooling on my pillow. I feel delicious and sleepy and wonder why I'm even awake at all. My brain is still half in my dream, fluttery feelings of pleasure still whispering in my ear. A soft knock on my door has me sitting up, holding my blankets up over my breasts.

"I'm up," I say, and watch as my mom pokes her head in the door. She's looking decidedly and adorably disheveled, wearing her sunglasses inside. Her bathrobe is askew overtop of her pajamas and she's only wearing one sock.

"Morning Sweetie, you have a visitor."

I look at the clock on my bedside table and note it's only 8:30 in the morning.

"I do? Who is it?"

"Your man Tate is back for more already." She chuckles, then clutches her head dramatically. Groaning, she shuffles away from my door leaving it open. I can hear her chastising herself as she shambles down the hall. I swing my legs over the side of the bed and pad across to my closet. I pull on the first dress I see, an apron style, linen number that has straps that cross in the back. It's cute without being too frilly and makes me feel like a Swiss milkmaid whenever I wear it. I twist my bedhead into a knot at the top of my head and head down to the kitchen, where I hear hushed voices. My bare feet are silent on the hall carpet, but I guess Tate's werewolf super senses will let him know I'm on my way down. When I walk into the sun-filled kitchen I smile. Tate is squeezed in on the end of the short bench in the breakfast nook, while Alma and my mom are spread out across the rest of the table, languishing in their hangovers.

Dad is at the stove prepping pancakes and Dennis is in Tate's lap. I lean against the door jam and grin at him. Gods, he's good-looking. His hair is clean and his eyes are glittering with happiness at me. He's wearing a navy henley and perfectly worn jeans today. I could eat him up, he looks so good. I watch his eyes shift to his Wolf's and realize he heard me. I blush and duck my head, then square my shoulders and lock my eyes with his. A dark, lopsided grin spreads across his handsome face and I watch as his gaze dips to my feet and travels all the way back up to my messy top knot. I can feel his eyes like a wave of warmth spreading over my whole body. His nostrils flare and his gaze jumps to my hand, then his bright eyes burn with heat as he locks his hungry gaze on me again.

Oh shit.

Oh *no no no*. I clench my hands and stuff them into the pockets of my dress.

18

Tate

My Mate pleasured herself last night. My desperate, hungry Wolf is practically beside himself inside me. When she comes down in her little milkmaid dress, I nearly have a heart attack. All the blood that's been in my brain, maintaining my conversation with her *parents and aunt*, jumps ship and hightails it to my dick. All words fail me.

She props herself against the doorframe from the hallway and smiles her sweet smile at me and I take her in. From her dainty bare feet, *(does she ever wear shoes?)* slowly up to her rumpled hair that she's clearly just tied up off of her slender neck. I inhale a deep breath to take in her scent and that's when I catch it. The sweet scent of her cunt is thick on her fingers and I know, *I know*, that she touched herself last night. Oh Gods fucking dammit all, she slipped her fingers into her juicy, hot pussy and made herself come. I'm teetering on the edge of delirium and have to grip the stool beneath my ass to hold myself in check. I know my Wolf is burning out of my eyes as I watch her realize what I'm reacting to. Delectable pink flushes up her chest and across her cheeks as she thrusts her hands into her skirt pockets. She opens and closes her mouth a few times, like an adorable little fish, and manages to produce a squeak. My chest is growling, low and deep and I can't take my eyes away from her.

"Good heavens, what's that rumbling?" Katrin moans, her head cradled in her folded arms on the table. "Is there a truck turning over out on the street?"

"Oh do keep it down, Darling, I'm sure it's our desperate stomach linings still waiting on Abe's pancakes to cure us." Alma mutters darkly. She lifts her head from her own hands just enough to wink at me and I chuff a laugh as the spell is broken.

I blink and shake my head to clear the fog of lust, and look back over to Ulla. She has her lips pressed firmly together and is dancing from foot to foot.

"I'm going to have a quick shower!" She peeps and whirls out into the hallway. My Wolf rumbles his displeasure at the idea of her washing her heady scent away, but I'm confident we'll be basking in it again soon enough. Ulla's scramble to hide her attraction to me is endearing. Like I won't know exactly what her body needs. My Wolf is so attuned to her that we'll give her everything she wants, anything she desires. I remind myself that this is new for her. I've spent my whole life as a werewolf, there isn't much about it that surprises me. But Ulla is an Earth witch, I'm sure of it. The way she communicates to animals is like a blinking arrow shouting it to anyone with supernatural senses. And as far as I'm aware, there aren't a lot of werewolves running around. We're literally a rare breed, so I imagine she won't have a lot of other experiences with us to draw from.

I settle into my seat at the table again, letting my muscles release the sexual tension thundering through me and tune back into the conversation around me. It's mostly a lot of groaning and muttering from the ladies, while Abe hums and clatters around at the counter next to the stove. I think he's enjoying making as much noise as he can while not being overly obvious about it. The scents of milk, flour and sugar dance around the warm space and I'm happy to be in the middle of it. My folks left when Seb and I were just cubs and our grandparents had taken us in. I don't remember much about them other than some feelings of connection I try to hold on to. It's hard to miss someone you don't remember, but the longing that's chased me my whole life would argue that you can. Gamma and Gramps did their best, but they didn't have the energy to really embrace all of our shenanigans. We know we're loved, that's never in question. But this lighthearted teasing being tossed around Ulla's family kitchen isn't something I grew up with. I like it. I want to roll around in it and let it rub my tummy.

"Honey, how much longer are you going to be bashing around over there, making the world's loudest pancakes? I'm sure I'm dying." Katrin wheedles. Her dark sunglasses are perched on her nose, her forehead creased in a frown. Her fluffy robe is pulled up high around her shoulders, blocking out as much of the light behind her as physically possible. Alma seems to be faring a little better, and I wonder if she has a hangover amulet that's keeping the worst of her misery at bay. Her smokey eyes are brighter than Katrin's and I suspect she's playing up her symptoms in solidarity.

"Drink more tea, my Love. It's one of Cora's blends and it always helps." Abe counters, not offering a timeline on carb delivery.

"Uuuugh the tea is so far away. Tate, would you be so kind as to help a foolish old woman?"

"Speak for yourself Darling, I'm in my prime." Alma chimes in.

"Pardon me, would you be so kind as to help a foolish, *perfectly prime* woman by making a pot of hangover tea? Happy Alma?" Katrin continues mulishly.

I smile and catch Abe's shoulders shaking out of the corner of my eye and scoop Dennis off my lap to attend to their suffering. The little kit prances and jumps up onto the table, Alma smoothly tucking him into her lap before Katrin catches on that the little beast had made it onto the tabletop.

These people are a well-oiled machine of love and friendship. The observation makes my chest feel warm and sweet, like a fresh cookie. I think of my own motley crew of family; Seb and the girls, even Aunt Jett, and decide we're doing alright. Now that Ulla has returned to Cora and Desi, we'll roll her into our little huddle like a cinnamon bun. She's the sugar to my spice and I realize with a rueful chuckle that I need to eat something before all of my thoughts turn into food.

I snag one of the hot pancakes while Abe isn't looking and inhale it as I look around in the cupboard for the tea. Inside are neatly stacked tins of Cora's specialty blends, all labeled in her tidy script. I quickly find the canister labeled "The Morning After" and hold it up to Abe. He glances over and nods, and I fill their silver teapot to the brim with steaming water. The scents of ginger, mint and rosemary join the buttery miasma already swirling through the kitchen and a sense of deep contentment fills me. My Wolf recognizes this place as home, filled with our new family, and he settles inside me with a sigh of relief.

19

Ulla

Y*ou are a confident, grown-ass woman Ulla Sinclair, and it's*
totally no big deal that your new boyfriend can tell you took
matters into your own hands.

I'm staring at my reflection in the bathroom mirror,
still a little foggy from my hasty shower. It was a *very embar-*
rassed, scrub everything you can reach as fast as you can shower.
My hair is damp and curling around my shoulders and my
cheeks are rosy. Although my flushed cheeks are more from
a ridiculous sense of chagrin than from scrubbing.

I've put on the same linen dress that I flung off of my
body as I hurtled in here, and paid attention to the underwear I chose to wear today. Based on how we react to each
other, it seems like a reasonable expectation that Tate may
see these later.

Oh Gods, I want him to see these later! Heat floods
through my body, pooling between my legs, and I groan.
My shoulders feel loose and my eyes are glassy. I look
drunk. Lust drunk in my parent's house! Alma is going to
have a field day with me when I go back down to the
kitchen. Or maybe not. Maybe she'll still be hungover

enough to let me squirm in peace. Oh who am I kidding? She'll eat me alive. She always knows. I still don't know how she knows what she does, but she always seemed to be one step ahead of us when we were younger.

I give myself a little shake and make eye contact with my reflection.

"You are a confident goddess of womanhood and you have a *very* sexy werewolf downstairs who clearly wants to have sex with you." Oh my stars, I do. He's so primal and visceral and the very idea of what he can do to my body sends licks of hot fire surging through my veins. I dance on my toes and shake out some more of my nervous energy. I may squeal a little bit too.

I hear a ping on my phone from my bedroom and throw myself onto my bed to check it. There's a new chat thread going between Cora and Desi that must have begun while I was in the shower.

DESI: **Girl Gang assemble! I want to hang out with my girls and we haven't had a date with just the three of us since our Ulla returned to us.**

CORA: **She only just returned yesterday, cool your jets Ace.**

DESI: **My jets will never be cool for you ladies, gimme all your time!**

CORA: ***eyeroll emoji***

. . .

CORA: **I'm actually very fine with this plan, I want this too.**

DESI: **Of course you do, we have lost time to make up for! We need to get all of the Tate details too. He glazed over like a holiday ham when he talked about her yesterday,**
    Mad Adorbs.

CORA: **Ew, your teenager is showing D, it's gross.**

CORA: ***barfing emoji***

ULLA: **HE IS HERE AT MY HOUSE RIGHT NOW AND I AM FREAKING OUT!**

DESI: **Alma is not hungover, do not trust her.**

ULLA: **Ugh that's what I figured.**

CORA: **Never trust my mother, she is an evil genius and her plots of world domination are nefarious and far reaching. Also, she loves to poke the bear so SHOW NO WEAKNESS.**

DESI: **She is a delight, just own your badassery.**

. . .

ULLA: **Aww! Thank you Desi, but I don't feel like a badass right now. I may have embarrassed myself more than usual just now.**

CORA: **TELL ME EVERYTHING**

DESI: **Tate could smell that she romanced her own stone.**

ULLA: **Jesus Christ Desi!**

CORA: **Yeah girl! You get yours!**

ULLA: **I have to go, He is HERE AT MY HOUSE and is eating breakfast with all of the parents and I'm going to literally die of mortification.**

DESI: **No you won't, my lovely Stroopwaffle, Tate is your Mate and werewolves love big.**

CORA: **Yeah they do. *side eye emoji***

ULLA: **I love you both and I am shutting my phone off now!**

. . .

I hit the power button on my phone and throw it into my little rucksack, along with my water bottle and a sweater for later. This dress is cute, but if the rustling trees outside my window are telling the truth, I'll need a warmer layer this afternoon.

I give myself a quick once over in the bathroom. My hair is nearly dry now and it's a frothy mess as usual, so I twist the front section away from my face and pin it above my ear. A swipe of lip and cheek stain and I'm as ready as I'll ever be.

I square my shoulders and take a deep breath. I am a badass. I am a badass. I can do this. I can walk into my own kitchen and be cool. Be *smooth.*

I debate trying to send a quick thought to Tate's Wolf but decide to just head down and see what we'll see. I'm not sure if we're ready for that yet. How is it even possible I only met him yesterday? It feels like I've known him my whole life, like we've always been together. The way he looks at me and the way my body responds to him is something out of a dream. He settles something inside me, but he also stirs things up. I bite my lip and smooth my dress down. My hands sliding over my hips feel charged with static electricity and I shake my fingers out to release the sparks.

I can hear my parents and Alma in the kitchen. And I hear Tate. His rumbling laughter swirls around my head like a glass of champagne, glittery and effervescent. I follow their voices and smile as I see them still at the kitchen table, finishing up the stack of pancakes that Dad made.

"There she is!" Dad exclaims as I step into the doorframe.

Tate's eyes are bright, watching me with an open expression of pleasure. As much as his hungry gaze sets my blood on fire, this guileless joy speeds up my heart rate in an entirely different way. He's looking at me like I'm the biggest present under the tree on Christmas morning. I can't stop the smile spreading across my face.

"Oh good lords. Tate, get up and take our girl out of here before your grins break your faces." Alma groans. Dad chuckles and slides himself out from the bench and kisses my cheek.

"Have a fun day kiddo," He says quietly. "You remember how to break a nose?"

I bark out a surprised snort and press my lips together and nod.

"Yeah Dad, right into the sinus cavity."

"Good," He swings around to Tate, "You take care of my girl today, she's more precious to me than all the stars in the sky."

"Yes sir, I know exactly what you mean."

20

Tate

She stands in front of me in that milk-maid dress and I feel like the luckiest fucker that's ever lived. She's looking at me with warmth and beaming anticipation and my fingertips tingle to touch her. My Wolf is purring his satisfaction inside me and her smile shifts to a dimpled grin.

Oh for fuck's sakes, the woman has dimples. All my charming and witty banter flies right out of my head and all I can do is stare at her. How can one person be so perfect? How did the universe wrap up everything I love into a single creature who looks at me like I'm a slice of chocolate cake? Because she is, her shining eyes are eating me up, and I want to lay down in front of her and give her a spoon.

"What do you want to do today?" She asks me. I have to shake my head to clear it from my mooning. Anything. I want to do everything with her.

"I thought we could go walk through McLaren park, the fiddleheads are uncurling and the trails are dry enough for you to take your shoes off."

Somehow her eyes manage to get sparklier and her smile even brighter. How does anyone see anything around her? She shines so brightly.

"That sounds perfect," She replies.

You are perfect. My Wolf wants to howl inside me and I can feel him vibrating to get out to the woods so we can shift and run with her.

We drive out to the Provincial park in comfortable silence. My Wolf is happy just to be near her and my lovely, mesmerizing Mate sends him calming thoughts the whole ride. It's like she can read my mind and we don't need to speak out loud. It's a little weird but also feels so easy. Like we've been doing this together forever. Actually, it isn't *like* she can read my mind. She *is* actually reading my mind. My Wolf. Whatever. It's fucking cool and just another tally in the Ulla Is Awesome column.

As we get closer to the woods, her body becomes more relaxed. I can feel her energy radiating off of her in waves while she sits quietly next to me in my old truck. Her scent swirls around me and settles my Wolf. He's so satisfied that she's nearby, and now that she's sinking into her own calm, my Wolf is even happier.

We get to the hiking trail and spend the whole morning wandering through the lush, green forest. The ferns are opening up all around us and I take in the familiar dips and valleys with new eyes. Ulla's connection and appreciation for the wildlife around her is palpable. It soothes my Wolf to be in this place that feels so magical with the one person who fills all of our empty spaces. We speak softly, as if the woods around us will wake up from the spell if we're too loud, and the hush feels like a blanket over the world.

Ulla took her shoes off almost the moment we arrived at the trailhead, and I'd happily swung her little pack over my shoulder once she'd neatly tucked her sandals inside it.

She's unencumbered and trails her hands over every leaf and branch she can reach. Her riot of white curls floats around her head and somehow manages to collect leaves as we walk, although I don't see her put them into her hair. It's as if the forest itself is crowning her with gifts, and she wears them like a queen.

As we crest the hill that takes us to the little waterfall this town is named for, the breeze shifts and Ulla's scent crashes into me. She smells like fresh green grass, crisp morning sunlight and sweet orange blossoms. She smells like *home*. I suck deep lungfuls of her into myself and let my Wolf roll around in it. He's unashamed to luxuriate in her and she laughs.

"I can hear his satisfaction from here," She says in her wind chime voice.

My Wolf's answering rumble moves through my body and I watch Ulla as her eyes grow dark, her pupils dilating in desire.

"Oh wow, I don't think I'll ever get used to this." She whispers.

I prowl over to her, closing the distance in a few long strides and stop in front of her. I'm so much bigger than she is and I don't want to loom, but I can't resist the pull between us. My fingers itch to touch her soft brown skin. She looks up at me, her dark eyes shining and her breath tickling my neck.

"I want to take this slow, but my Wolf has designs on you." My voice is gritty, and I clear my throat.

"Can I see him?" She asks.

My Wolf purrs inside me and she smiles, hearing his pleasure and having her answer before I can speak. She reaches out and runs her fingers along the side of my forearm, tracing a line on my skin down to my hand and interlaces her fingers with mine. My stomach fills with butterflies and my whole body breaks out in goosebumps. I can't deny her anything she wants. I was born to serve her. It doesn't hurt that my Wolf wants this too.

I nod, hand her the backpack, and take a step back. As much as I want to always be touching her, I also don't want to freak her out by shifting into my Wolf while she's touching me. We're still getting to know each other. It feels like we've known each other forever already, but I don't know what kind of movies she likes, her favorite color, or if she'll be squicked out if her boyfriend turns into a Wolf right in front of her. The usual first date stuff.

"He'll never hurt you, you don't have to be afraid of him." I say, my voice a little hoarse, my pulse pounding in my ears.

"I know, I trust him. I trust you, Tate."

I don't understand how she can be so chill about this. Werewolves aren't something that a lot of people are usually blasé about. But here she is, her sweet face shining up at me with all of her trust right there, shining in her eyes.

"Would it be helpful if I give you more space?" She asks me. "I can perch on that log over there and then you can spread out. Is he very big?"

My Wolf and I both chuckle darkly at that, and I have to bite my lip to keep from making a dick joke.

"Oh my Gods Tate! You're ridiculous, that's not what I meant!" She bursts out laughing and I join in with her. My Wolf is besotted and she wants to see all of us, so I close my eyes and let him rush to the surface. Shifting for me is like relaxing a tight muscle. I keep him locked tight inside of me most of the time, so when we shift and trade forms, it feels like releasing the tide or opening the floodgates to my true self. I let him flow over me and feel the electric tingle spread over my whole body. I roll my shoulders forward and as I crouch down to the ground, my Wolf's fur ripples over me, and I'm no longer standing in front of Ulla on two legs, but four. I shake out my Wolf form and take a deep breath in. My sense of smell is pretty great when I'm in my human shape, much better than a regular human. But as a Wolf it's like I can see the scents around me. Everything is crystal bright and Ulla's scent hits me like a battering ram. She's warm and spicy, fresh and delicious. I stand very still as I watch her take me in.

21

Ulla

Tate as a Wolf is enormous. He's so tall I bet his head would reach my shoulder and I can probably ride him like a horse. Jesus Murphy, he's bigger than I expected. I mean, I thought he'd be big, but holy shit.

My pulse speeds up and I sit very still, taking him in. His shaggy fur looks soft and thick, practically gleaming golden in the slanting light that's breaking through the trees above us. I'm a good six feet away but I can feel the heat pumping off of him from here. He stands very still, like he's trying to let me set the tone of this first meeting and a surge of affection flows into me.

"I will stand here until you are comfortable, Ulla Mine."

Oh! His voice is right in my mind! Tate's Wolf chuffs a small laugh and ducks his huge head. I hop off the fallen log I'm perched on and take a step towards him.

"Your voice is very clear, you sound like Tate, but different."

"I am Tate, but different. We are the same soul with two shapes. We are very lucky."

I smile at that. His voice and thoughts are so dear to me already and I wonder at the magic of the Mate bond.

"It is a rare gift, we are very pleased to have found you so soon in our life span. This means many years ahead of us together. Very pleasing."

"I'm pleased too," I say, and I mean it. This connection with Tate came out of the blue, but it doesn't feel awkward or wrong. It actually feels very, very right and I trust the instinct that draws me closer to him.

"Can I touch you?"

Tate's Wolf purrs deep and low and I watch him close his eyes.

"That will also be very pleasing. I wish to feel your hands in my fur."

Well then.

I take a few small steps towards him and bring myself right in front of his muzzle. We're nearly eye to eye and I marvel again at how big he is. He gently and slowly sits on his haunches and lets me close the distance between us.

"I will hold very still for you Little One."

I smile and reach my hands out. I softly stroke the length of his head from his eyes to his ears. His rumbling increases, like a giant cat purring in pleasure, and I stroke his ears to the tip. He's so soft! I run my fingers gently over his ears again and I feel a thumping start up all around me. Is that… my heartbeat? No, that doesn't feel right, my heart's beating faster than this new sound. I blink and look around. And see it. The Wolf's tail is thumping against the ground with pleasure. Tate's Wolf is wagging his tail!

I can't stop a giggle of delight from escaping me and I rub his muzzle and run my hands over his shoulders. He isn't scary or intimidating to me at all. I'm sure if anyone else ran into this giant Wolf they likely won't feel quite so relaxed, but everything about this feels good to me. That's the most amazing thing about all of this, every time I consider the Mate Bond and rationally think it through, I just feel at ease. Contentment. Every time I look at this situation I've found myself in, I just feel a pleasant and familiar joy.

"You're so beautiful. Your fur feels so soft under my fingers." I whisper to him. Tate's Wolf slowly pushes his long muzzle into my hair and I feel him inhale against the skin behind my ear. Cascading flames lick over my whole body and I tremble. But not in fear. Never in fear. Heat travels over my body, starting at my fingertips as a light fizz and rushing through my body to pool in my center. I feel it settle low in my belly and I hear my breathing change.

"I, um." I stammer.

Tate's Wolf catches the change in my breathing too, and his big body stills. His tail stops thumping against the ground and he holds himself as still as a statue.

"Ulla Mine, I can scent your hunger. But I do not wish to frighten you with my own."

"I appreciate that." I squeak. I'm panting now, my body's reaction to the energy swirling around us making my voice sound low. I've curled my fingers into the soft ruff around his ears and I watch, awestruck, as the fur shifts into Tate's soft, scruffy hair and he's suddenly kneeling in front of me in my arms. His eyes are bright, his Wolf shining in them and he stares so deeply into mine, that I could fly into the stars and not notice. We're both breathing slowly, soft and hot, the sensation of his breath on my lips burning across my skin like wildfire. I tighten my hands in his hair and without any conscious thought I pull his head down to mine and we're kissing. Kissing like we haven't seen each other in years and the only thing holding ourselves together is each other, and our breaths shared between us. His long, strong arms hold me tight against his broad chest and I wrap my arms around his head and we kiss each other to stay alive. We kiss each other like we'll never see each other again. His mouth over mine feels like a prayer, like devotion, like all of the kisses in my life leading up to this were just a tease. A hint at what's possible. *This* is what kisses are supposed to be. Heat and need and lust and fluttering, keen, desperate *feeling*. We press our bodies as tight against each other as we can. There can be no space between us, only our bodies crashing and pushing towards each other. I can feel the Wolf inside him, sending me all of his need and desire and it dials my own up even higher.

I gasp out loud when Tate pulls his mouth away from mine and presses open mouth kisses along my jaw, his teeth scraping against my throat and down my body. I wrap my legs around his waist and grind my hips into his. He groans, low and deep, and I feel it deep inside myself. Oh Gods, I want this man.

"Tate, please." I whimper.

He lowers me to the ground, the soft moss under my shoulders feels cold and jarring under my heated flesh but I lose myself to Tate's mouth against my neck. His big hands shift over my hips and run down to my knees and then up under my dress. His fingers are rough and calloused. I briefly imagine him working with those hands, earning those callouses. Then his fingers brush against the lace of my underwear and all thoughts flee before the onslaught of electric sensations and I'm only feeling.

I whimper again as I try to catch my breath. His mouth is still moving lower down my chest and my breasts feel heavy and aching. He brings one hand up my hip, over my breast and drags the front of my dress down. He kisses and licks and then, *Jesus Christ*, he sucks my nipple into his hot mouth and I cry out, writhing under him. I can feel his sharp teeth scraping against my skin and his hot tongue swirls over my tight nipple. His other hand fists my underwear and tears them away from my body with a jolt. I gasp again as I feel his thick fingers slide up my thigh and then into my slickness. I buck my hips for more. More. Oh Gods I want *all of this*.

22

Tate

Ulla's scent is driving my Wolf wild. She's soft, sensual perfection. Every breath hitched, every whispered moan is a song in my heart. I want to devour her. The feel of her stiff nipple against my tongue and my hand covering the rest of her lush breast makes me feel dizzy. The taste of her skin is intoxicating. I can't stop my other hand from roaming down her round hip and grazing the skin of her thighs. Oh Gods her heat is pulsing, pushing outwards from the apex of her sex and I growl deep in my chest. Her hands are tight in my hair, fluttering over my shoulders, moving around and grasping me wherever she can. Like she can't touch me enough. Gone is the timid, gentle creature we had breakfast with. My touch has transformed her into a Goddess full of want and hunger. Fucking hell, I love it. I love *her*. Holy shit, I *love* her. It's way too soon for love right?! It can't be love already. My Wolf disagrees, he's madly in love with her and has no qualms about it. Why should I? The magic of the Mate bond is powerful and as far as I know, never wrong. Mates are written in the stars, meant to be. I let myself feel how I feel and accept that the force between us is bigger than the two of us. Flames of lust and affection surge over me, down my spine to flare in my balls, filling me with a delicious ache.

She grinds her hips against my throbbing dick and I slide my hand all the way up to her panties. Godsdamnit, I feel delicate lace and my mind nearly explodes. I tear it away from her heat and nip at her breast with my teeth and she gasps. I slip my hand up and up her soft, dimpled skin and into her pussy. I groan again.

"Oh Gods, Ulla, you're so wet for me." I rasp around her flushed tip. I lick and move my mouth over to her other nipple, kneading her breast as I slip one finger inside her hot cunt.

She arches her back and her ragged breathing takes on a new rhythm.

I pull my mouth off her delicious tit with a pop, and move my body over hers to kiss her mouth. I suck and bite at her lips and she moans her sweetness into my soul. She kisses me back, hard, her tongue tangling fiercely with mine as we battle towards her orgasm. I add a second finger into her pussy, stretching her, pumping my fingers and feeling her tight walls clench around them. I slide my thumb over her clit and press. Her whole body pulls tight and her cunt clasps and sucks at my fingers, and I nearly explode my release into my jeans. Ulla's gorgeous body twitches and shivers as she rides out her orgasm, my fingers still slowly moving inside her to stretch it out as long as I can.

Finally her body relaxes, all of her muscles letting go as she slumps into my arms and lets her head roll back onto the soft moss underneath her. Her ragged breathing slowly evens out and I pull my fingers out of her body and bring them to my mouth. She watches me as I suck her juices off my fingers one by one and my eyes roll back into my head.

"Holy shit Tate, that… that was…"

Her taste explodes on my tongue, filling my senses and I growl, my Wolf pushing at the surface again.

"Let me know when you've caught your breath." I say, my voice gritty and deep, even in my ears.

"What?" She whispers. She shimmies her upper body up onto her elbows, her incredible breasts spilling out of her dress. I crawl myself up over her again and press my nose into her neck, breathing her in. I rub my cheek against hers and whisper, "I want to lick your cunt and hear you come again."

She whimpers and grabs my face. She kisses me deeply, pouring herself into it and I grip her tight. I fist my hands into her dress and hold on for dear life.

I feel a hot huff of breath on my back and the hair on the back of my neck stands to attention. What the fuck? I pull away from Ulla's kiss and frown. Her eyes flutter open, then she inhales sharply and her eyes fly open wide. I feel a stomp behind me and hear a huff of breath again and slowly turn my head around.

Staring at us, not even three feet away is a doe. She watches us with curious eyes and stamps her foot again. We have an audience actually. I look around past the doe, behind Ulla and all around us. There are animals *everywhere*. The doe is just the only one brave enough to get so close. I count several squirrels, rabbits and other furry small creatures along with a whole aviary worth of birds. Plus the doe and some raccoons? What the actual fuck?

"Uh, is this normal?" I hiss.

"This has never happened before." She whispers, her eyes darting around to catalog the voyeuristic menagerie.

"I've also never had sex in the middle of the woods though, so maybe?"

I keep my body still over hers, shielding her from view as much as possible. I don't know if that's necessary, but my Wolf is feeling possessive and he isn't willing to let anything near our Mate at the moment. I can feel his low, rumbling growl start in my chest and I shoot a glance over the assembled peanut gallery. I notice the greenery around us is leaning towards us too. It's as if Ulla is the sun and the whole forest is leaning closer to soak in a little bit of her warmth. She pulls everything in towards her. I smile down at her and her eyes crinkle at the corners.

"Perhaps we press pause on this and finish our walk back into town?"

She presses her lips together and looks around us. She closes her eyes and I feel a deep calm spread over and past me. She's telling the animal assembly that the show is over and slowly they start to pull away and disappear into the woods. The young doe is the last to go and as we slowly stand up, brushing the dirt and moss out of each other's clothes, she watches us with her liquid eyes and twitches her nose. Ulla slowly steps closer to her. My Wolf is not in support of this, the doe is big enough that she can do some serious harm if she spooks. But my fearless little Mate gently lifts her hand to the deer's muzzle and strokes her hand down the animal's soft nose. The doe pushes her nose further into Ulla's hand like a pony would and my Mate croons at her and pets the wild animal. After a few silent minutes have passed, Ulla presses her forehead to the deer's and then steps back. The animal turns to me, seems to realize I'm an apex predator, and shoots off into the green. The rustling trees around her exit are the only evidence she'd just been here.

"So you're essentially Cinderella without the evil step family and drudgery."

She laughs and shakes her head.

"I don't have mice and birds dressing me in the morning, but they do tend to come around more for me than the average bear."

Her smile is rueful, and I wonder again what the story is behind the shadow of sadness that passes through her eyes.

"I'm getting better at controlling it, but it tends to get out of hand when I'm distracted." She bites her lip, tucking that one corner under her teeth and my cock pulses.

"Next time I distract you properly we'll try it indoors," I say. I want to throw her back down into the moss and finish what we started, but I don't want another audience of Disney characters. Once is enough.

23

Ulla

"Next time I distract you properly we'll try it indoors," He says, his voice raspy and deep with desire. I have to breathe through the zip of surprise and pleasure at his words. I've had some weird animal encounters over the years, but this is a whole other level. I expected Tate to be put off after this. Even for me, opening my eyes as I nearly come out of my skin to see a whole audience peering at us is new ... I've also never had sex in the woods, so maybe that happens every time? I shudder a little at the thought. As much as I appreciate my gifts with animals, there are some things that should remain sacred. And Tate making me come all over his fingers and mouth? Is one of those things I really want to experience again. And again.

The few boyfriends I dated in the past always ran when things got Dr. Dolittle on me. Like, cut and run. I'd hoped that Tate would be different, he's a werewolf after all and that's definitely different for me. But when I'd opened my eyes and seen all the furry faces staring at us, my orgasm still thrumming through me, I assumed that he'd freak out and run too. But he isn't. He wants to *"distract"* me again indoors.

"Next time?" I ask, my voice small and hopeful.

His eyebrows furrow a little, and he tilts his head slightly. I feel a little push on my mind and realize the Wolf is pushing thoughts at me. I let them in and gasp at the ferocity.

"You are MINE, Little One, now and forever."

"Really?" I ask, breath hitching.

Tate takes a step towards me, slow and sure. He runs his big hands up my arms from my elbows to my shoulders and cups my cheeks.

"I'm yours Ulla, nothing will scare me away from you. Have men you've dated in the past not stuck around after they learn of your gifts?" His voice is low and soothing, his frown deepening when he asks about other men. Like he doesn't want to ask about previous boyfriends, like he's jealous.

"Is that why your eyes are sad? Do you think I'll leave you now?"

My eyes fill with tears, and I feel them slide down my cheeks. Tate softly brushes them away with his thumbs, caressing my skin and sending shivers through my body.

"They all leave." My voice is broken, breathy. "Men, friends. Only Desi and Cora have kept me."

He growls but I'm not afraid. He growls because I've been hurt, not because he would ever hurt me. I hear his Wolf in my mind and I know they'll never, ever hurt me.

"I won't leave you. You've lit a fire inside me and I'm yours, body and soul. I see you, Ulla Mine, and I love what I see." I bring my hands up over his, he's still softly rubbing his thumbs over my wet cheeks and it feels so, so good. My voice is a little stronger now,

"You do?"

He smiles then, his sharp teeth flashing and his eyes shining.

"I really do. You're kind and brave and loving. You accepted my Wolf like it was no big deal and we're yours, forever. You're my Mate, and I'm your very willing servant." He wags his eyebrows as he says that and I snort a laugh. He's broken me out of my self despair and he did it by just being him. By accepting me as I am and being his own damn self so I can accept him too. And I do. As strange and as sudden as our connection might be, I accept it, embrace him.

This bond between us feels like a gift and I'm no longer willing to let fear or doubt stop me from enjoying every minute of this magic with him. I step towards him and he lets me shift our bodies so that I'm wrapped in his arms. I press my cheek to his broad chest and squeeze him in a tight hug. His big hands run up and down my back, sending warmth throughout my whole body.

His erection is a scorching brand against me and I think about taking him into my mouth. I like the thought so much I send an image of what I'd like to do with him through my mind to his Wolf. He groans and I feel his knees tremble.

"Ulla, you don't have to do that, it's enough to make you feel good." He grits out, his voice like sandpaper.

"I want to," I say, running my hands over his back and down to his ass. His glorious, tight ass. Good grief, his body is a delight. He groans again and pulls me up his body, dragging me against his length and crashes his mouth against mine. I wrap my legs around his hips and we kiss each other, a little desperately. He keeps one hand under my butt to hold me up and his other arm snakes around my back to crush me against him. I wrap my arms around his neck and shoulders and we make out like teenagers. It's heaven. I can feel his Wolf vibrating with pleasure in his chest, it feels really good pressed up against my breasts. They're still full and aching, the sensations swirling around me start to coalesce in my core.

"Mmmm I can smell your need Ulla Mine, *Gods*, you smell so good." He growls. I only whimper in response, my breath coming in heaves as we grasp at each other. I'm distracted by the feel of a cool rustling behind me, and I pull away from Tate's lips in a daze. I turn my head to look behind me and right on par with how this whole encounter is going, the leaves from the nearest tree are tangling in my hair. As if the tree itself is reaching towards me. Tate laughs and I turn my face back around to look at him. His eyes are glassy, his mouth is pink and swollen from our kisses.

"I think this is our cue to head back into town." His chuckle is rueful and I press my lips together. I nod and he slowly releases me to slide down his body. I feel his hard length running down my center and realize with a groan that he did it on purpose. His mouth hooks into a wicked grin as I watch and I have to blink away the dirty thoughts that flood my mind.

"You're bad." I tease.

He adjusts himself through his pants and I watch unabashedly. That big dick is mine now and I can't wait to get my hands on it. His Wolf shines out of his eyes like a flash of heat and I realize he heard me.

"So are you." Is his pleased response, and I bob my chin at him even as a flush creeps across my neck. His laughter rolls over me like goosebumps and he reaches for my hand. I happily place my hand in his and we head back down to the trail to head back into town. We've both had enough nature for today.

24

Tate

My Mate is something else. I spend the rest of the day with her, getting cock blocked at every turn. But even though my dick feels like a steel rod and my balls might be permanently blue after today, I've never been happier.

Once we make it back into town, we pop into the bakery, where Sela fawns over Ulla and packs us a bag of sweet, doughy heaven. Walter came out from the back kitchen and regaled us both with tales of wooing Sela, who clucks and blushes whenever he shares a glance with her. Ulla is utterly charmed by them both and we spend more time there than I expect. We leave with Ulla and Sela having secured a tea date to connect more and my girl is beaming with happiness.

After that, Desi corners us in the courtyard and winks at me as she pulls Ulla into their shop to try out some new dresses she'd just brought in. I knew I'd lost my Mate to sartorial bliss when Cora pulled out a chair for me to sit and wait in. The giggling and exclamations of delight that surround me make me smile, and I settle in with the bag from the bakery to enjoy the show. I don't know how long we end up spending with Desi and Cora, it feels like hours but it could've only been forty-five minutes. All I know is, Ulla is wrapped up in happiness and laughter and I want her to have all of it. Anything that makes her smile, I'm happy to support.

Seb wanders in after the girls had made Ulla try on every single dress they'd brought out and they're now whispering with their heads together. Every once in a while I'll catch Ulla's eye and she lights up like it's Christmas morning and smiles at me like I'm her own personal elf. Who am I fucking kidding, I'll put on striped tights and suspenders for her any day.

Seb chuckles as he watches the women spin around each other, each of them talking over the other like they all need to say something vitally important at the same time, their voices getting higher and their words faster the more they agree with each other. It's fucking adorable and I could watch them all day long.

"Cora's very happy to have Ulla back in town," He says in his quiet way. I think about what Ulla had said earlier, how Desi and Cora are the only friends that stuck. I resolve to do my best to share her as much as I can. My Wolf isn't keen to share her at all, but even he recognizes how happy she is right now, and keeping her feeling good is our primary goal. If I'm not doing it with my mouth or hands or cock, I'll make sure she's surrounded by our friends. Luckily this little crew of weirdos is also my Pack, so we'll just pull her into the madness and let her stew in it.

"Me too Man, what a trip this is," I say, still smiling. Seb grunts pleasantly at me and grabs another chair. We settle in to watch our Mates be adorable and let our Wolves enjoy a quiet moment together. The volume that's created by our little pack is surprisingly high, even Cora is getting worked up with the giggles, and it makes me so happy. The more time I spend sitting and watching them enjoy themselves, the more content my Wolf is. Seb's too, evidenced by the small smile on his mouth. His shoulders are relaxed and I realize with a little zip of awareness that he needs this too. We're all benefitting from the new addition to our pack dynamics and I let the fog of smug contentment wash over me. My Mate is filling us all up with her light and it's good.

We spend the rest of the day with said hooligans, and by the time I bring Ulla back to her parent's house, she's glowing with joy and tired from laughing all day. We hold hands as we walk up to the front porch and stand under the light. I know this woman is it for me. Even without the bond scorching between us, I *know*. She's everything I never realized I wanted. I reach my hand up and tuck a wayward flower back into her hair. She didn't start the day with them, but she's collected a crown of blossoms that dances around her head like butterflies. It's just something about her. Maybe it's her Earth witchiness in action, but I've yet to see her without something green and blooming in her hair. I love it.

She smiles up at me and bites her lip. I've noticed she does it when she's thinking about kissing me. Her gaze drops to my mouth and my own quirks up in a grin.

"You can kiss me whenever you want, you know," I say. Her soft cheeks flush with color and she presses her lips together as she chuckles.

"Is it that obvious?"

"Your secret's out, you can't resist me."

Her laugh erupts out of her like champagne bubbles and I pull her into my arms. I cup her face with my rough hands and bring my lips to hers in a soft kiss. She sighs into my mouth and then licks my lower lip. I groan and hold her closer to my body. My dick has been achingly hard all day, but it's practically thrumming for her now. She wiggles her hips against me and I hear her breath hitch as she feels my erection press into her. We've been doing this dance all afternoon. I know she wants to get her hands on me, having my Wolf catch her dirty fantasies all day long is a glorious tease. So I know she wants me as much as I want her. But I'm not going to claim her on her parent's front porch, any more than I was going to do it in their garage last night. Gods, had that only been last night?

"Tate," She whimpers into my mouth. I inhale my name from her lips and slide my tongue into her mouth and against hers. This kiss is languid and deep, searching and slow. Her hands move up over my chest and into my hair. I love that she tightens her little fists into my hair when she kisses me. It feels like she has to hold on for dear life because my lips on hers are too much.

"Can I see you again tomorrow?" I breathe against her mouth.

Her groan of frustrated need is music to my ears. I feel the same way leaving her, but I can hear her Dad on the other side of the door shuffling around the house and I don't want to embarrass her if he decides to investigate why she hasn't come inside yet.

"Yes please." She finally huffs out.

I rub my thumbs across her cheeks and kiss her again. A light kiss of promise and a good night.

25

Ulla

Can you get lady blue balls? It must be a thing, because I definitely have it. I thought I was a reasonable and calm person, but this feeling throbbing through me, that no amount of deep breathing or thigh squeezing seems to alleviate? It's starting to piss me off. But it also makes me feel dizzy with anticipation. I've taken care of myself several times over the last week, to no avail. Oh I'm getting myself off, that's not the problem. The problem is that almost as soon as I give myself a little relief, I think of Tate again; his rumbly voice, his thick fingers on my hips, his blazingly bright smile… And I get all tight and frustrated again! We've been dancing around each other all week, kissing and touching and generally being *that couple*, but every time we get close to finally sealing the deal, something crops up to foil our dirty, sexy plans.

That day last week in McLaren with the animal audience was just the first of several mood killers. There's also been my parent's walking in on us in my bedroom; I need to get a lock on my door. Or better yet, look at getting my own place. There were bees in the back garden, *that* was surprising and also a little terrifying.

Since engaging in all of the hormone driven make outs with Tate lately, my magic has been getting wilder. I can feel the edges of my control trembling the longer it goes on and I'm not entirely sure what to do about it. The strength of my gifts have been steadily increasing since I was a teenager. Puberty really amped things up and I had to develop new strategies to manage it. But the flare of power that's ignited inside me since connecting with Tate feels different. More intense. We'd been making out in the back of Tate's truck when I visited him at General Pawspital yesterday, and Daisy broke out of her kennel again and jumped into the back with us, bringing three other dogs and an alpaca with her to peer into the windows at us. I'm starting to wonder if we'll ever have sex. I'm not holding back, I'm very invested in going all the way and enjoying everything that his hungry eyes and big, stiff erections promise. But we're going to have to get serious about finding some alone time soon before I sexually combust.

Today I have an interview at the local branch of the library. I've been in town for nearly a month now and it's time to put down some roots. There's no way I'm not staying in Eliza Falls, I have so much here and I just need a job to make it official. I've been putting out feelers all over town, everywhere from the pet store to bagging groceries. I even had an interview at the university just outside of town, but the position is part time and is geared more for grad students. I already have my masters degree and it feels wrong to usurp a student who needs that job more than me. I can stay with my parents as long as I need to, I'm just itching to branch out and settle in on my own. With my own place, a door that locks, and a bedroom I can utilize for seducing my hot as hell boyfriend. Then Sela had mentioned her cousin was retiring from his position of library manager and that they were looking for someone to take over that role, and I nearly fell out of my chair. The manager position is only one step away from director and is what I'd been doing at the branch in North Vancouver before my contract was up and I moved my life here. I'd immediately zipped home to collect my CV and called to set up an interview.

I choose a knee length skirt and camisole for my interview. It's comfortable and put together enough to look professional and still feels like me. A long linen jacket goes over top and I'm as ready as I'm going to get. I twist my hair into a knot behind my left ear and pin a sprig of rosemary blossoms I poached from the garden into it for luck.

Mom and Dad are tucked into the nook enjoying their second cuppa when I whirl through the kitchen and they beam at me.

"My goodness Ulla love, you're a vision this morning!" Mom says.

"Thanks Mom! I'm excited and nervous for my interview, this job would be perfect."

Dad clucks at Suzanne, who'd slid herself into view on top of the fridge.

"I got her Dad," I say. I reach my hands up to her and she smoothly moves her long body down my arms and across my shoulders. She likes to curl up on top of the fridge in the mornings and nap in the heat that pumps up from the motor, but it stresses my dad out every time. Mom smiles as I transfer Suzanne over to Dad's shoulders and he whispers sweet nothings at the python. Rolling her eyes at my dad's obvious affection for the snake, she leans over to kiss his cheek and then pulls herself out of the window seat.

"I have a walk with Alma this morning, I'm going to

get myself ready to go. You'll charm the pants off the library director today sweetie, I have no doubt." She kisses my cheek too as she sweeps past me and I press my lips together in a smile. These easy moments at home have been so soothing. It's filled up a part of me I hadn't realized was empty while I was living on my own in the city. My parents have never pressured me to live my life any particular way, but I know they miss me when I'm not nearby. Being an only child means I get to enjoy a lot of their attention, and I know how much I mean to them. Being back at home with them isn't something that'll last too much longer, but settling here in the same little town means I can see Mom for tea dates and help Dad with whatever zany animal mishaps he gets himself into. My smile deepens as I realize I'll be able to do that when I secure a permanent job here. I have enough savings to tide me over for a few more months if I need it, but getting this job will mean I can start looking at finding my own place. There are a few adorable little cottages around town that fit my lifestyle perfectly. Something close enough to the woods so I can soak up the green and hear the rustling leaves in the morning. With a little patch of yard I can tend to and grow. The more I think about it the more I like it. Picturing my own place makes me think of Tate again. Everything tends to swing back around to him. But this time I think about how nice it'll be to have my own place to have him over to. He'll come in after working at the studio with Seb, smelling like wood chips and oil, I'll rub his shoulders and he'll kiss me in the kitchen.

"Well now kiddo, you're blushing and I'm going to take a stab in the dark and say it's not because of your interview," My dad chuckles. *Oh good grief*, I'd slipped away into fantasy land again. I shake my head and press my hands to my cheeks.

"Sorry Dad, got a little lost in a moment there."

He smiles and gives Suzanne a gentle rub over her body. She's draped over his shoulders still with her head tucked behind his ear.

"It's nice to see you feeling happy. I'm not going to pretend that it's just because you get to see my handsome mug every day."

"It's a big part of it, Dad." I step over to him and kiss his cheek, stroke Suzanne and pull myself up to head over to the library. This interview is a big deal, and I'm going to get this job.

26

Tate

Running through McLaren Woods is one of my favorite things to do. Letting my Wolf out and giving him free rein to stretch his legs and feel the earth beneath his feet give both of us a sense of peace and satisfaction.

Since Ulla has lit up our lives, we haven't taken the time away from her to get a good run in, but today she's occupied in town. She's set herself up with an interview at the library and won't be free to hang out until later today. I'm so pleased she's putting down roots here. I'll follow her anywhere, but being able to keep my little Pack together too is the best outcome.

Seb and I had driven out to the south lot first thing this morning and shifted as soon as we confirmed there were no other early morning hikers out today. He's a quarter mile away, his Wolf tracking the perimeter, and I let my mind wander as my Wolf thunders happily through the underbrush. He's a big golden goofball a lot of the time. Seb is alpha and we're happy to let him do all the alpha-type things he feels he needs to do. A lot of it is instinct alongside knowing where we are in the pack. A pack of two don't have many power struggles when we're both comfortable with the status quo. Seb's been my alpha for as long as I can remember and I'm more than happy to fall in line. There's never been a time when my instincts have rebelled against Seb's Wolf. He's a good leader, even as grumpy as he usually is.

Having this time to run and think, I allow my thoughts to play back to what Desi saw in her vision a few weeks ago. Her premonitions are sometimes vague and open to interpretation, but not all of them. This one seems to fall somewhere in between, the riddle of it poking at me like a tongue on a sore tooth. The threat is unclear, but the menace feels all too real. I'm unable to stay away from Ulla for too long, so Seb and I have settled on a system where he runs the perimeter of town every day, scenting for anything unusual, and I keep close to town and my Mate. Cora has taken it upon herself to snoop around town and generally make a snarky nuisance of herself. It's mostly cute, and her new obsession with tracking all of our phones means that she's often sending us on localized errands. Desi's still playing it cool, not giving us anything else to go on, other than we still have time to figure it out. She's pretty good at letting these things play out, but the thread of tension I sometimes feel through the bond I have with her tells me she's not as calm as she'd like us to believe. None of us has found anything unusual so far. So we're left wondering and worrying, and acting like we're not. It's frustrating to not have any definitive antagonist, but a relief to be doing something. Anything.

It's easy to get lost in Ulla's sweetness and smiles. There's such an energy of innocence around her, that keeping my mind on the things Desi said all those weeks ago is getting harder and harder. It's challenging to maintain vigilance for something as intangible as smoke, an unknown threat with no real boundaries or timeline. Add on top of that the driving need to claim Ulla and settle my Wolf, and I'm a kettle ready to boil over.

We see each other nearly every day, but the most ridiculous and untimely interruptions continue to cock block the shit out of things. Her tranquility is a balm to my Wolf's restlessness. It's the only thing satisfying him enough to not have lost our ever-loving minds by now. I know Seb waited nearly a year after scenting Cora before claiming her and completing the Mate Bond, and I have so much more respect and admiration for my brother now. I'm unraveling fast, the edges of my control getting more ragged by the day. Only her voice in my head is holding me in check. I honestly have no idea how Seb managed to not flip the fuck out without Cora all that time. Ulla's ability to communicate directly with my Wolf is as rare and magical as she is lovely. Which is saying something since she's the most wonderful carbon-based creation to ever live.

I shake my big body and continue to lope through the woods, letting my Wolf get as much of a run in as he needs. Seb's presence in our mind is a beacon to the north end of the park and his thoughts through the pack bond remain chill. My Wolf nose scents the usual forest citizens, nothing out of the ordinary.

I itch to get back to town so I can be closer to Ulla again. I know she'll be busy for most of the morning though, so I push through the desire to turn around and run to her parent's backyard. Their home is close to the edge of the woods and it would be easy to slip into their space and hover like a stalker, but that's not me. I trust Seb's nose and my Wolf's senses to alert us to any danger. Nothing will keep me from my Mate if she's threatened. I'll tear the world apart to keep her safe.

27

Ulla

F or a week and a half I stewed in my own juices as I waited to hear about the library position. They interviewed another candidate as well, a lovely older woman I've seen around town. She works at the high school library and her resume looked intimidatingly thick. So I've second-guessed myself all week and driven Dad bonkers as I fretted. Suzanne and Dennis both gave me a wide berth and it was only Tate and his delightfully distracting qualities that allowed me to be half reasonable at all.

But after all of my stress, I received a call from the head librarian confirming that I got the job, and now that I've had a chance to settle in, it's as wonderful as I expected it to be. I know librarian doesn't scream sexy, but Gods above I love it. Samuel Baker, the director, is like the grandpa I never had. Both of my grandfathers passed away before I was born, so I never had a lovely old man who wears sweater vests and teaches me how to bind a book properly. But Samuel did that on my first day and I'm wildly in love with him. I'll be managing the little branch here in Eliza Falls and it's so quaint and cozy. I'm already brainstorming new ways to organize everything and updating the system. A little thrill dances down my spine every time I think about all the color coding I'll get to do in the future.

I've been working nearly full-time for the last two weeks now and other than the restricted access to Tate, I've never been happier. My days are full of books and research, learning this sweet space and managing the programs we offer. My evenings are spent on romantic dates with the hottest man I've ever laid my horny eyes on. He's spoiled me rotten every night we've gone out. We haven't had a night alone together yet, I think our series of ball busters has forced us to slow down in the ripping each other's clothes off department. But I'm so ready to get to it. Oh my sweet heavenly stars am I ready.

I'm wrapping up my last few tasks at my desk, in my very own office, when I feel the air shift around me. I always leave my window open for the breeze and to listen to the little garden just outside. There are often little creatures out there, birds and mice, occasionally a cat or two, and it's reassuring to be able to listen in on the regular sounds of nature. I blink to clear my eyes as I look up from my computer and I luxuriate in the caress of the breeze across the back of my neck. The air is getting warmer as we step closer every day towards summer and my favorite time of year. Summers here growing up are the highlight of my childhood and I'm so excited to spend my first season back here for good. Just knowing I'm here for the foreseeable future and that I have roots to tend to, fills me with an immense sense of satisfaction. It coils in my belly and settles my nerves. I feel a tug on the bond I share with Tate and turn my head towards the sunlight streaming through my window behind me. I can tell he's close even though the bond hasn't been completely sealed yet. I think we need to get to some serious claiming soon to tighten it up. Cora mentioned the bond becomes even stronger once I've been bitten and we get biblical and I *can not* wait.

I'm squirming in my seat when Tate ambles in. Jesus Murphy and all the chocolate cake, he's a delight for the senses. We've been all over each other for nearly a month and I still feel a thrill whenever he looks at me. And right now he's looking at me like he knows what I'm thinking. A slow smile spreads across his beautiful face and I chuckle to myself because he does know what I'm thinking. His Wolf flashes behind his eyes and I send them both a burst of my anticipation and delight. I may also send them a visual fantasy of what I want to do to his big cock tonight and I bite my lip as I watch Tate stutter step and blush.

"You are a vixen, Ulla Mine." He growls at me as he stalks around my desk and drops to his knees beside me.

"I've been thinking about you all day," I reply, my voice breaking a little.

"Have you now?"

I nod, not trusting my voice. He runs his hands up my calves to my knees and gently spreads them open and slides his body closer between them. The heat radiating off of him is like a physical force of its own, beating against my skin. He smooths his hands over my kneecaps and then slowly, with the barest touch against my skin, collects the hem of my skirt and inches his fingers up my thighs. His touch is soft, his skin hot, and he bunches the fabric while his hands move higher. My breath is coming in deep drags of air, my chest verging on heaving like a damsel, and I embrace the feeling. He makes my whole body come alive with the barest touch, and right now his intention is as clear as the day is long and I'm absolutely here for it.

"Are you wet for me?" He grits out, his voice getting rougher by the moment. I shift my hips closer to him, bringing my ass to the edge of the chair. Trying to get closer to him. He continues his slow torture with my skirt, inching it up my legs. I spread my thighs a little wider, brushing my knees against his hips. He groans low in his throat and then his hands are sliding up my thighs even higher and I feel his fingertips brush along the edge of my panties. I clench my hands tight on the arms of my chair, I want to feel his touch and I don't want to distract him from what he's doing. It's too good.

He looks directly into my eyes as he traces along the outer edge of my vulva, where my inner thigh connects to the sensitive flesh, and I begin to tremble. I'm panting now, big and deep, and I lick my lips.

"Your pussy is so hot, I can feel how wet you are through your panties." He whispers. He's leaned in far enough now that I can feel his breath against my skin and I make a strangled sound. He chuckles and his hands slip around my hips, away from where I want him. I feel his fingertips dig into the flesh of my backside. He tugs me forward abruptly, and now my core is pressed up firmly against his thick length, and my eyes roll back into my head. I arch against him and begin to rock my hips to rub my desperate pussy against his cock through his jeans. He groans as he leans forward and we're kissing in my office and I can't stop and I need this man deep inside me.

"Tate I want…." I moan into his mouth.

"I know, Gods I know. I need to claim you, Ulla. I can't hold back any more." His hands are becoming fiercer, holding me against him, and I rock my hips, feeling the delicious friction exactly where I need it. I hear a scrabbling and a thump behind me and Tate is suddenly jerking away from me. I open my eyes to see a crow has pushed its way into my office through the window and is staring at us intently.

"Jesus fucking Christ!" Tate exhales. He still has one hand on my ass and he runs the other through his hair. The crow blinks at us and cocks its head.

"Uh, let's go to your place and lock all the doors and windows," I say.

"This is definitely the weirdest way to make sexy plans." He grumbles. I can feel his cock twitching against my center and I have to close my eyes and hold my own groan in.

"I can honestly say this is new for me too. But she wants to watch and I'm not sure how I feel about that," I say, nodding to the crow who's still staring at us, while she hops from foot to foot on my desk.

"This isn't as scary as the bees, but way worse than the deer." He mutters. I snort and try to act cool while I disentangle my legs from around Tate's hips in a way that says confident and cool with this and not squirming in embarrassment. He lets his hands linger on my legs as I step down from my chair and he watches my skirt with hot eyes.

"Let's go to my place right now."

Yes please.

28

Tate

My Wolf is practically snarling in pleasure as we drive Ulla back to my apartment. Her scent is swirling around us in the small cab of my truck, making me nearly delirious with need. I came very close to driving my dick inside her in her office just now and even in my addled desire, I know that's a bad idea. Our first claiming should be somewhere we can spread her out like a buffet and feast on her. She deserves to be worshiped, and I intend to do just that.

I glance over at her. She's biting her lip and her legs are restless like she can't hold still, like her arousal is driving her just as wild as it's making me. I can taste her scent in the air and hear the slick of heat between her thighs as she squeezes them together. I groan and she shoots a look at me so full of hunger and understanding that I'm tempted to pull over to the side of the road and suck the juices off her sweet little cunt right now.

"Oh Gods, Tate. Your Wolf is so loud." She moans. She fists her skirt in tight hands and rolls her head back against the seat.

"Just get to your place in one piece, I can hold out." Her voice is ragged, practically a gasp, and I scowl at the road as if my glare can make it shorter. I shake my head to clear it and focus on driving the truck. I breathe through my mouth to try to block her scent and keep my Wolf in check. He's prowling and fierce now that he knows we'll be fully claiming our Mate soon.

It feels like the longest drive home of my life, but we're finally out of the truck and stumbling up into my little cottage. I have enough sense left in me to lock and dead-bolt the door as Ulla strokes my shoulders and all across my back as I draw the curtains.

"Make sure the windows are closed." She whimpers and I break away from her to do a quick sweep. Nothing will stop me from taking her to bed and plunging deep into her depths this time. My home is small and I have the windows all locked and the curtains drawn in short order. I nearly stumble to a halt as I swing my big body back into the living room. The light is muted through the curtains and a hush has fallen over the world.

She's here, panting and gorgeous, her dark eyes nearly black with her desire, and I groan deep in my chest at the sight of her. She runs her small hands over her thighs and as I watch, she draws her hands up over her hips and her perfect, lush tits, and fists the front of her dress. The fabric pulls her flesh tight as she twists her fingers into it and I can see how hard her nipples are.

"Jesus Ulla, you're so fucking hot." I grit out. My teeth ache as I watch her lips part and she inhales a ragged breath as she trembles in front of me. I've moved towards her without even realizing it, her gravity pulling me in, and I stand in front of her prepared to sacrifice myself at her altar.

"Please, Tate," She whispers. "I need you inside me."

My Wolf snarls and I let it rumble through my chest. This woman, this Goddess, needs me, and I'm powerless to resist her anymore. I reach my hands up into the nimbus of her hair, sliding my hands into the silky strands. Her eyes flutter closed, as if my touch is setting off sparks inside her and she can only *feel* as I stroke her hair away from her face and grip the back of her neck. I lean down and slowly, softly, rub my cheek against hers. I rub my nose behind her ear and she shudders.

"I'm going to take you to my bed now," I whisper, barely speaking at all.

"Yes."

"I'm going to lay you back on my bed and peel your skirt up your thighs."

"*Yes*, fuck, I want that." She breathes.

I force myself to move slowly. She's trembling and panting as I slowly move my hands down her neck, over her shoulders. Over her back and down her spine. I splay my fingers out across her lower back and she gasps as I slide my big hands down to her ass and lift her up. She fists the front of my shirt and wraps her legs around my hips. Oh Gods, I can feel her hot pussy against my aching dick, and I groan. I press my face into her neck and slide my tongue across her skin. She's so fucking soft everywhere, all of my hard edges are held in her body and I nip at the flesh where her neck meets her shoulder. She makes a strangled sound in her throat and throws her head back.

"Tate, please, yes," She shudders, and I walk us into my bedroom.

I lay her down in the middle of my bed and hold myself over her. Her hands travel over my chest and up my neck, her fingers in my hair sending embers of fire racing straight to my dick.

"No more holding back Love, I need you too much." I

grind out. Her dark eyes are glassy with need but she holds my gaze. Our foreheads are pressed together and her breath mingles with mine.

"I see you, all of you. You're mine, forever." Her words skate over my skin like water and the bond flares bright between us. My Wolf is so close to the surface that I have to close my eyes and force him back. She waits, knowing he's so near, giving us the space to be ourselves, and I'm never letting her go. Never letting anything come between us. She's my salvation and my dreams and my Mate. I blink my eyes open and she's here, her beautiful mouth crooked into a grin.

29

Ulla

Tate's big body over mine feels delicious. He's so warm and solid, his legs braced in between mine and his strong hands in my hair. I feel enclosed by him, safe and loved and cherished. There's never been any doubt in my mind as to how he feels about me. The magic of the Mate bond sends me pulses of his feelings and glimpses of his thoughts. It's all love and wonder and desperate, aching need. His Wolf is fighting to get close to the surface. We've had too many almost claimings for him to be able to hold on much longer. I can feel him pacing at the edges of Tate's control. I breathe in their mingled breaths and close my eyes. I send the Wolf calm and surety. This is it. I accept them and I want them and we've locked all the fucking windows and doors. We're doing this. His Wolf is still there, still close, but he's calmer now and I open my eyes to see Tate gazing at me with love in his eyes. We haven't said the words to each other, but it's there. I see it in his gaze and I feel it in the way he's so tenderly holding my face in his hands. He's slowly brushing his thumbs against my temples, stroking my hair away from my face and I wonder if he even knows he's doing it. His bright hazel eyes are hungry, but his expression is soft. I grin up at him, and his answering smile is like a punch to my core. This stunning specimen of a man is mine. And we're about to make this a permanent situation between us because I know, down to my very bones, that there's no going back after this. Once the bond is sealed, with us very likely fucking our brains out, there's no other man for me. And he's been very open about how the Mate bond works and I have no illusions and zero regrets. In fact, I can't wait to bind myself to him and his Wolf for the rest of my life.

I arch underneath him, pressing my breasts into his hard chest and he growls down at me. I love it when he does that. I can feel the vibrations all the way to my toes. He presses his hips down into me and I wiggle mine to tease him. He shifts his big body so that he can nudge one of his lean legs higher in between mine and I shamelessly rock my center against his thigh.

"Jesus, Ulla." He groans into my mouth, right before he kisses me deeply. I open to him and sweep my tongue against his in a hot dance of desire. I grind my pussy against his hard muscles and the friction, in combination with his searing kiss, sends me exploding into an orgasm so fast that I keen into his mouth. I twitch and shudder my climax and he keeps kissing me, so hot and so deep that I may never put myself together again. He's rocking his big body over me, letting my slick pussy clench and pulse out the last tremors of my orgasm and I blink my eyes open as I feel his hand trace my breasts and move down to my hip.

"You're so fucking hot, I love watching you come." He finds the bottom of my skirt and starts to slowly drag the fabric up my bare legs. His fingers feel scorching, my skin on fire where he's touching me. I squirm beneath him, feeling my arousal spike again. I fumble with the buttons on his soft shirt and he quickly sits up on his knees and pulls it over his head. His hair is messed up from my hands tugging on it and his eyes are liquid pools of hunger. He's never looked more beautiful. I reach up and run my hands over his abs and chest, the crisp hairs tickling my fingers. His breath is heaving and I grab the button of his fly and pop it open, rubbing his thick length through the denim while I do. He practically snarls as I unzip him and see the tip of his cock pushing up out of the top of his black boxer briefs. Heat and wetness flood my panties at the sight and I gasp.

"Pull your dress off." He grits out. His voice a rumble of gravel.

I bite my lip and shimmy myself out of my dress, throw it on the floor without thought and push myself up onto my elbows. I can feel my nipples pressing against the lace of my bra and the air feels cool against my soaking panties.

"Take your pants off." I counter. His eyes flare magnificently darker and I watch as he slides off the bed and stands to push the worn jeans down over his hips, taking his boxers with them so his glorious cock springs free. Oh holy hellfire, his body is a Godsdamned testament to the wonders of the universe. He chuckles darkly and crawls back over me.

"He heard that thought didn't he?" I ask him, wry and breathless.

"We like it when you ogle us, Ulla Mine. Shall we show you how much we like your body?" I can hear the shift in Tate's voice, see his Wolf watching me through those hazel eyes, and I find it so incredibly hot that they're both claiming me at this moment. The rumbling in Tate's chest deepens and he slowly moves up my body. He props his upper body up on one arm, that hand fisting in my hair, and his other hand skims down my belly and into my panties.

"You're so fucking wet for me." He whispers, his voice practically dragging over my skin with how gravelly it is. I don't even have time to nod before he tears them off of my body.

"Gah! That's two now!" I breathe.

"Just stop wearing them and I won't have to rip them away from your sweet cunt." Now I'm the one groaning, his words stoking the fire inside me even more and I rock my hips up into his hand. He rubs his face against my breasts, his breath hot and ragged and I need him inside me. My core is clenching on nothing and I'm desperate to feel him stretching me open, making me his in this primal way.

"Please, *please,* Tate, I need you," I manage to say, my voice raw and sultry. He takes his thick cock in his hand and rubs the swollen head through my slippery folds. It feels so good and I buck against him, no longer able to control myself.

"You like that?" He growls at me, "You like it when I rub my dick in your hot pussy?"

Jesus *fucking* Christ, I love this man.

"Yes!" I snarl back, "Now fuck me."

His eyes flare and he stills for just a moment.

Then he pushes that gloriously thick length into me and I cry out at the stretching, fearsome pleasure of it. He pushes into me with an aching tenderness, slow and inexorable. His body trembles above me and I open myself to him, tipping my hips to take him as deep as I can. He's so big that I can feel every solid inch of him pressing against my inner walls and I throw my head back at the beauty of it. My hips rock against him and he grinds his cock deeper into me, rubbing against my clit and I nearly come out of my skin.

"Gods YES, oh fuck, you feel so good." My voice is squeaky and straining and I grab his ass to hold him against me. He groans and presses his face into my neck and slowly slides out, until just the tip of him is still inside me. I whimper as he chuckles, the sexiest sound I've ever heard in my life. His hands are in my hair again, his thumbs stroking my cheeks as he gazes deep into my soul. I'm surrounded by him, pinned by his hips and sheltered in his arms braced on either side of my shoulders. He drags a thumb across my lips and his other caresses my neck and I let a sob of desperate need escape me.

"Are you with me Sweetheart?" He whispers.

"Yes." I breathe.

He strokes himself back into me, deep and sure. I rock my hips up to meet him and we're coming together in a force as powerful as the tides. In and out, over and over, he pushes into me and I meet his every stroke. He holds my gaze, his hands on my face gentle, and we breathe each other in, in the most intimate dance. I pull one leg up and over his hip, taking him in deeper and he groans and loses his rhythm. He starts to move faster, rocking into me with more desperation and it's *everything*. The sounds of our bodies crashing together and his fierce expression fill me with an emotion that I can't describe. Flames of ecstasy shoot to my fingers and toes and I lean into it. I arch up to kiss him, the dual sensations of his slick tongue against mine and his hips pistoning against my core sends me over the edge. I'm coming so hard I don't know where I end and he begins. His kiss travels down along my jaw, and down my neck. My throat is stretched tight and I'm sobbing my orgasm into the soft light around us as he continues to fuck me with everything he has. I feel a bright sharpness at my shoulder, a burn that sends my body soaring into excruciating pleasure. My cunt is squeezing him so tight and I feel my inner muscles fluttering around his length as he suddenly stills over me, roaring his release into my neck. The bond between us flares bright, pulling taut between us and I feel his joy, effervescent and burning hot in my own chest.

30

Tate

H oly shit.
        That was… that was…
Holy fucking shit.

I can't think straight. I can feel Ulla underneath me, her cunt still clenching around my dick, who's a Gods-damned champion and is still half hard. We're both pant-ing, sweat slicked all over our bodies and I've never, in my life, felt as happy and fucking blissed out as I do right now. It's like claiming Ulla has given my Wolf a full body high and he's tripping balls right now. I kiss my Mate, *my Mate*, all over her face and neck, my mark on the tender flesh of her shoulder already healing, peppering her with affection wherever I can reach her without pulling out of her sweet, blessed heat.

"Tate, gah!" She wriggles underneath me, laughing.

I roll us over to the side so I can wrap my arms around her and she slings a leg over my hip. I'm still inside her and I hold her lush curves against me tight, still pressing kisses to her hair. I can feel the bond between us glowing bright gold and pulsing, her thoughts trickling over me in snippets. My Wolf is too dazed and satisfied to parse any of them out at the moment. She burrows her face into my shoulder and I allow myself to just wallow in this contentment. I feel like all of the years spent quietly yearning for connection have led me to this moment, this woman. A sweeping sense of peace fills me and I realize that Ulla is my home. She is the piece of me that's been missing for so long. She mutters something into my armpit and I have to roll her back just a little to hear her properly.

"What's that, Love?"

"I like what you did there. A+ effort. All the gold stars." She grins at me, a little dazed, and I feel like the luckiest son of a bitch that's ever walked the earth. I chuckle and she gasps as my cock twitches inside her.

"Oh wow, are you.. is that..?" She starts, and I pump my hips against her. She moans and throws her head back as my lengthening dick strokes inside her and I palm her perfect breast, rubbing her taut peak with my thumb. She arches her body, pushing her hips against mine as I continue to slowly fuck her again, and she hitches her leg higher over my hip taking me even deeper inside her slick channel. I squeeze her tit, the delicious flesh spilling out of her lacey bra, and pinch her nipple as I watch her shudder. It drives my Wolf utterly mad. He's growling his satisfaction inside me and my whole body is thrumming with the vibration. But I keep my movements slow and deliberate. I want to draw out every push and pull between us and I need to make her feel all of the love that's coursing through me. I lay my other hand over her luscious ass cheek, spreading her wider, and continue to stroke my now achingly hard dick in and out of her heat. I groan and grit my teeth, the pleasure already spiking at the base of my spine. Her fingernails scratch along the back of my arm that's still kneading her breast and I lean forward and pull her soft flesh into my mouth. My teeth scrape against her skin and I flick my tongue over her hard nipple and she cries out. I suckle harder at her flesh then and can feel her cunt spasming around me and I can't keep up the slow pace anymore. I pump into her hard and fast, forcing her climax to the next level and her whole body goes rigid as she rides it out. The sounds of our bodies slamming together, deep and wet, draws my balls tight against my body and I explode inside of her. I roar my release as she takes all of me, and we're both left shuddering and panting in each other's arms.

Her body feels so perfect wrapped up around mine and I send contentment through the bond. She practically purrs and her limbs go loose as she sinks into a thoroughly fucked and satisfied sleep. I chuckle low in my throat as I realize she literally passed out from fucking me and hold her close. With my perfect Mate in my arms, safe and asleep, my Wolf knows a joy so bone-deep that I let it wash over me and swim in it. This is what we are meant to do. My sole purpose in this life forevermore is to please and love and cherish this woman, keep her so well satisfied that she only knows joy. My Wolf chuffs his agreement and we both let the magic of claiming Ulla sweep us into sleep as well, her body tucked against ours, our breath mingling together and the Mate Bond pulsing brightly between us.

31

Ulla

I wake up to hot, rough hands sliding over my hips and a big warm body spooning me. I like this.

"Mmm, morning you," I mutter. My voice sounds hoarse and scratchy, and I realize I made a lot of noise last night.

"Yes you did, we intend to do that again." Tate's voice is low and growly and sends shivers deep into my core. His Wolf is present. Oh wow, yep, I'm definitely liking this.

I shimmy my bum backward a little and come into contact with a very thick, very hot erection. I shiver, antici- pation swirling in my belly. We got *into it* last night, memo- ries of just what we did to each other bubbling up to the surface of my thoughts, making my core clench. Tate's rumble increases and his arms tighten around me, his hips starting a slow grind against my ass.

"I can tell how wet you are already, Ulla Mine," he growls into my hair. I shiver again, pushing my hips back into him to encourage the delicious grind he's started, and reach my arm up and around so I can grab his hair. One of his big hands travels up my belly, sliding over my bare skin to cup my breast. The other skates low to cup my mound, one thick finger sliding into the seam of my sex. I inhale sharply, the flesh under his hands is tender from last night.

Tate suddenly stills, his breath stops.

"Ulla, did I *hurt you* last night??" His voice is strained. His Wolf bristling inside him, pushing at the edges of his control. I marvel at being able to sense all of that very briefly, before I send a wave of calm and love to them both.

"You most definitely did not. I enjoyed every second of being claimed by you, and claiming you right back if you'll recall," I say lightly.

"I heard how tender you felt just now, I'm so sorry." He starts to pull away and I grip his hair tighter and hold on.

"Don't you dare pull away from me, I loved everything about last night and I love waking up wrapped up in you. Yes, I'm a little sore, but it's so good. It tells me we needed each other so desperately, and I don't regret a thing."

His breath fans against my ear. I'm fisting his hair still and holding his face close to mine. I send my satisfaction through the bond and let my arousal flood my thoughts. I also send an image of what I want to do with him right now and I feel him shiver against my back.

"Ulla, Love, I don't ever want to make you hurt, for anything." He grits out.

"The only thing that hurts is the empty ache inside me," I whisper. I press my ass against his length and he groans. I spread my legs wider and hook my top leg up over his hip, opening myself up to him. In this position I'm completely exposed; it feels vulnerable and sexy and my heart rate starts to increase.

"Touch me, feel how hot and wet I am for you." I plead, my voice sounding breathy even in my own ears. His big hand slides back over my mound and my breath catches as he slides his finger back into my folds. I'm slippery and hot, and my pussy clenches around his finger when he slowly slides it inside me.

"Jesus Ulla, I can feel your need in my belly." He groans into my ear and I moan out loud.

"Yes, Tate, please." I'm panting now, desperate to feel more of him inside me. I'm still holding his head close to mine and he nuzzles into my neck. His hand on my pussy swirls in my juices and he pulls that big finger out and then slides it back in again. He slowly fucks me with his hand and I shamelessly grind against his palm. His other hand squeezes my boob and I keen into the pillow. He adds a second finger inside my channel and the subtle stretch feels so, so good.

"Yes please, oh Gods this feels so good. I want more, Tate!" I whimper. He shifts behind me and then I'm spread open even wider, his hips still grinding against my ass. Now I'm fully open to him, and he explores my breasts and nips at my neck. He pulls his fingers out of me and spreads my wetness all over my pussy, circling my swollen clit as I moan again. He holds me open like this while he pushes his thick erection against my wetness and the tease is so good.

He slides himself through my slick folds, coating the swollen head of his cock before rubbing it against my entrance. He's still massaging my breasts with his other hand and I'm chasing an orgasm that's just out of reach.

"Do you need my dick inside you, Love?"

Oh Gods yes I do.

"Yes, yes Tate, please." I manage to whimper.

He pushes inside me, slowly and relentlessly, until I'm stretched tight around him and he's pressed as deep as he'll go. I can feel him so deep in this position and I heave deep, panting breaths as he starts to move, sliding his big cock out nearly to the tip and then slowly all the way back in. I arch my back and try to take him deeper, and he groans low in his chest. His hand over my pussy begins to move again and he swirls his thumb over my clit. It's all too much, the sensation of him filling me up so perfectly, my legs spread open so wide and his thumb circling over my sensitive nub makes me gasp and I pump my hips against him. My climax thunders through me and I cry out his name, shuddering all around him, and feel his pace increase.

"Fuck, I love watching you come on my cock." He grits out, never stopping his hand on my clit, forcing my orgasm to stretch out, the waves of it crashing over me again and again. The slide of his length through my tight cunt becomes erratic, his own release not far behind mine. I squeeze my pussy around him and he jerks his hips, the slapping of our flesh together an erotic soundtrack to this glorious moment and he stills, groaning deep into my neck. His teeth graze the sensitive flesh behind my ear and I come again, a surprise explosion that sends me over the edge and I cry out.

Dazed and heaving, we both lay together trying to catch our breath, the sweat on our skin making goose-bumps erupt all over me.

"We should do this every morning." I gasp out. Tate chuckles against my back, and he rubs his stubbly cheek along my neck and shoulder. I wriggle and laugh at the tickle of his whiskers and he squeezes me tight in a bear hug.

"That's a plan I can get behind," He says. His growly voice is music to my ears and I squirm again as he thrusts his hips into my ass again. The man is still, somehow, impressively hard and the slide of his cock inside me sends shivers of need down to my toes.

"Oh no you don't, I need to go to work!" I giggle breathlessly.

He relents and I untangle myself from the sheets and his arms. We're both a sticky mess from our lovemaking, last night and this morning. Sweat mats my hair and our mingled releases make my legs feel slick. Tate's eyes grow dark when he notices it and he stalks me to the bathroom just down the hall. I laugh and let him chase me into the shower where we spend a little too much time soaping each other up and he licks me all over. All over. I debate calling in sick so we can spend the day entirely wrapped up in each other. But I've only been at the library for a couple of weeks and it feels a little too soon to be playing hooky with my boyfriend. Instead, we flirt our way through a quick breakfast, never taking our hands off each other and having the nicest morning I think I can ever remember having before.

32

Tate

B efore I drop Ulla off at the library for her shift, we make a pitstop at her parent's house where she dashes upstairs to change into a clean dress and I spend a couple of awkward minutes with her folks. Her mom smirks and titters, but her dad just glares at me while he holds Dennis, both of them growling at me a little. I'm not entirely sure how to approach the whole hanging out with my girlfriend's parents thing this morning. I feel like up until now, Abe and I have had an easy camaraderie, but this morning he doesn't seem interested in having me around. I know I'm properly dressed because Ulla made sure we were decently presentable before we left my place. But something is rubbing him the wrong way and I'm not sure what it is.

A commotion at the front door signals Alma's arrival. Katrin mentioned the two of them were going shopping today, when Ulla and I had first arrived. Alma sweeps past me with her usual aplomb and stops just short of dancing around me.

"That's a charming love bite you have there, O'Connell." She sings in a stage whisper. Oh for fucks sakes. I blink and feel my cheeks heat, squirming uncomfortably as Abe's glare manages to get frownier. Katrin laughs out loud as she grabs her purse and elbows him in the side.

"Come now Love, Tate's a good man, we know this. We also know what it's like to be fresh in love… or don't you remember that first Easter weekend with your parents?"

I watch Abe's expression soften as he looks over at his wife and the two of them share a conspiratorial look.

"She's still my baby girl." He harrumphs. Katrin sighs patiently and kisses his cheek.

"Yes she is, and always will be. But she's also a grown woman with a Mate of her own, so let them be. I'm surprised they held out as long as they did."

I snap to attention at her words. Ulla and I haven't told them about my werewolf nature, and I'd assumed they had no idea. I blink and manage to keep my mouth shut while I desperately try to guess how much they know and how they feel about it. My Wolf is pacing inside me, my sudden flare of anxiety pushing him close to the surface with his hackles raised. I take a couple of slow, deep breaths to regulate myself and let his ears pick up anything that Katrin and Abe might give away.

"Relax Darling," Alma purrs in my ear. Jesus, I'd forgotten she was right behind me.

"I'm super relaxed." I lie. She rolls her eyes at me and tucks her hand onto my forearm, like we're strolling along the promenade.

"Ulla has been their daughter for twenty-six years, and I've been Katrin's dearest friend for much longer."

My head swirls and I have to blink to stay focused on the issue at hand. There are a few easter eggs in Alma's words.

"Do they know *exactly* what I am?" I ask her as quietly and as subtly as I can.

"I don't believe so. But they do know that those of us lucky enough to be… extraordinary, often Mate for life. It's not just shifters who corner that market, my Lamb." Her voice is smooth and unhurried. She has no qualms about having this conversation so close to Ulla's parents. But I'm less comfortable with it.

"I need to talk to Ulla about this and how to approach what we say. It's one thing to Mate another witch and have some idea of what to expect from them. It's quite another to Mate a Wolf and all the pack magic that comes with it." I mutter. Katrin and Abe have moved to the kitchen while Alma and I are still standing on the landing at the bottom of the stairs. I can hear Ulla dashing around above us, her light footsteps dancing.

"You're a lovely Wolf and a lovely person, Tate. The only concern the Sinclairs will ever have is how much you'll cherish their daughter. And you and I both know that this will never be an issue. Be easy, Darling. And consider wearing collared shirts. My goodness, my sweet god-daughter has some sharp teeth it seems." She chuckles, her voice rich and traced with love. I have to blink again, because I think I've just realized that Alma might love me.

I feel really lucky to have had the childhood that I did. I was pretty small when our folks left, but I never really felt alone or unloved. Seb has always been there, a dependable and reliable fixture in all of my memories. I suspect that he took on more of that role than he really needed to, just to make sure that I felt safe growing up. I don't remember much of my parents, so the ache is vague. I know Seb struggles with it, that he's been searching for something that might lead us to them. He thinks I don't know what he's up to, but I'm aware that the "traveling" we did before settling here in Eliza Falls wasn't just to develop our characters. He's been quietly looking for them for years.

Gamma is a formidable woman, fierce to her very bones. I always feel valued and I know that she loves us. But showing her emotions isn't something she's comfortable with. I think Granddad is the only one who knows what she really feels about anything. Seb is... well, he's Seb. I know in my bones he loves me, but he's cut from similar cloth to Gamma. He feels the feelings, but showing them is harder for him than it is for me. I've always worn my heart on my sleeve, whether I'm happy or sad or madder than a hornet, everyone around me knows it. Luckily for everyone around me, I'm generally a pretty laid-back guy, my moods leaning heavily towards the positive.

So this realization that someone who's the right age to be my own mom, and who is now technically my brother's new mom, might love me? Might love me and show it? This is a landslide of feelings I'm more than happy to swim in. I look down at her, and she's looking up at me with her knowing gaze. I grin, all teeth and crinkly eyes, and she smiles back.

"Ulla is mine, Cora and Seb are mine. You are mine too Darling. Don't you forget it."

I laugh and scoop her up into a bear hug. I'm spinning her around the landing when Ulla skips down the stairs. Her smile is bright and her eyes have questions, but she lets me squeeze the breath out of her godmother without interrupting us.

"Alright now, that's quite enough Precious. Go take our girl to work." She tries to sound exasperated, but I can see the pleasure in her eyes. I kiss her cheek before I scoop Ulla up for similar treatment. My Mate laughs and lets me spin her and I stage whisper over my shoulder to Alma as we head outside.

"I love you too Mama Bear." She rolls her eyes and shoos me off with her hand.

"Go on with you, you ridiculous man. Save your sentiments for your Mate."

But she's smiling and I hug Ulla tighter and take her to the library. Where my beautiful Mate is the *head librarian.* I suddenly have to focus on putting one foot in front of the other as all the blood rushes from my brain to my cock. This is a fantasy that I'll never get over being my new reality. Ulla tickles the hair behind my ears and I focus my gaze on her.

"Your Wolf is sending me some ideas Babe. Do I need to get my reading glasses and track down my sweater sets?"

Jesus fucking christ. I groan out loud and spear her with a hungry look. She gasps and blushes. Her core floods with heat, I can sense her arousal spike through the bond, and I'm sorely tempted to take her back to my place.

"Oh no you don't! I want to go to work!" She says, breathless but determined.

"Then to work you'll go, but we're revisiting this talk of glasses and sweater sets. Very soon."

"I like this plan." She squeaks as she scurries to the passenger door of my truck and hops in before I can catch her.

33

Ulla

Time is traveling in a strange way these days. My weekdays are filled with research, books and settling myself into my role at the library. It's everything I want in a job; the people are lovely, the building is adorable, and the books are all around me. Eliza Falls has a surprisingly full collection of Arcana history. For such a funny little town, there are a lot of serious books about magic. It's like an arrow from the universe pointing me to where I'm supposed to be. My research over the last few years has led me down such fascinating rabbit holes, bringing me here to this new collection of history books. There are even memoirs of real witches! It's thrilling to be able to add them to my list of books to be devoured. We witches often hide in plain sight. Although the more I see of this town, the more I suspect there might be fewer humans than supernaturals after all. I mean, Sela *has* to be a Kitchen witch. Her bakery is literally magic.

While my days are filled with fascinating research and getting into the nooks and crannies of the library, my nights and weekends are filled with Tate. My insatiable,

172

beautiful, magnificent Mate. The sex we've enjoyed since he finally, officially claimed me, has been the most incredible sex of my life. Sometimes it's silly and fun, other times it's heavy and laden with intensity. The man can bring it. Oh stars above, I get all twitterpated whenever I think about it. Which is a lot. Oh boy is it a lot. I'm very glad I have my own office at work.

It's been nearly a month since we started this sexy thing between us, and the summer Solstice is creeping up fast. There's an annual fair lined up for the weekend of the actual Solstice. It falls on a Saturday night this year. This town has an event for all of the Pagan traditions alongside some of the more conventional religious holidays and it's so lovely and welcoming. I missed the Spring Equinox Picnic and Egg Parade. But I heard about it from the pre-kindergarten Story Club. Sounds like a good time for the under ten set.

There's a Solstice bonfire scheduled for Saturday night, the town staff taking family schedules into consideration and making the events a weekend-long festival every year. It's all pretty sweet. My dad mentioned he went to it last year and it was an impressive bonfire they set up in the field behind the fire station. The parking lot gets cleared and a dance floor is set up off to one side. Tate's Aunt Jett is the ringleader of a ragtag gang of older citizens who attempted to streak a few years ago apparently. The police chief had to get involved and now they all wear nude body suits to get the whole dancing naked around a fire vibe. I can't wait for this year!

Tonight however is game night with Seb, Cora and Desi. Desi arranged a game of *Dutch Blitz* a couple of weekends ago and it was hilarious to watch everyone attempt to beat her. She has the unfair advantage of being able to see what's coming up in the deck if she concentrates, and watching Tate try to distract her while Cora swore her frustration like a sailor, had us all in stitches for most of the night. Even Seb was laughing openly at everyone's shenanigans. We'd set up the game in the little courtyard behind the shop. Desi has her apartment above the store and the courtyard has become our de facto headquarters now that the weather is warming up. A little raccoon had meandered up halfway through the evening and I ended up sneaking her bits of my snacks while the rest of them snarled affectionately at each other.

I'm spending less time at my parent's house now that Tate and I are basically inseparable. It feels wrong to sleep without him and my dad is still a bit grumbly about "boys in my room" which is as adorable as it is annoying. I think he'd be less against it if he realized that Tate is literally never going to leave. I imagine his human perspective will have him struggle to understand how serious Tate and I are so quickly. I know I'll have to explain just how secure I am in the knowledge that Tate is my forever to them soon. But it's just so nice to be wallowing in the Mate bond right now. I consider some options for explaining to my sweet human parents that their daughter's boyfriend is a werewolf. I wonder if Sela can write that on a cake?

Sighing, I finish organizing the papers on my desk and re-stack the books I've been pouring over while I wait for said werewolf boyfriend to arrive. Thanks to the bond with his Wolf, I'm able to "hear" them coming before they actually arrive. It's a handy little trick and I'm able to have everything put away by the time my hunky boyfriend ambles into my office.

"Hey Love," He drawls. Good Gods, I love that grin. "Are you ready to save the world tonight?"

"Sounds dramatic," I reply, coming around my desk to slide my hands up his hard chest.

"Desi's setting up a game of *Pandemic*, the expansion pack she ordered has arrived. She's feeling pretty positive about our chances this time."

I laugh, picturing Cora's furrowed brow the last time we played this game. She didn't like that we'd lost in only two turns and had gone into her game mode, which is a little terrifying. Even when we were kids, she had a competitive streak bigger than she was. I think she's happy to have the O'Connells to play with now, since both Desi and I aren't very competitive. Plus we've started looking at cooperative games to play for game nights, to make it a little easier on everyone. Cora is intense at the best of times, but game night really brings out her freak flag.

"Sounds fun," I say, reaching up onto my tip toes for a kiss. He brings his lips to mine and I feel the now familiar embers of heat lick over my skin. I smile into the kiss and he nips my lip with his sharp teeth. Sometimes, when he's feeling particularly wolfy, I notice that his canines are a little longer than usual and I don't know what it says about me, but I *really* like it. It makes me feel like a sultry, huntress-type person and it's a little thrilling to know he's all mine.

"Are you all done here for tonight?" He asks.

I give my office a quick once over and nod. My boss has already left for the evening and I'd tied up the loose ends I was working with before Tate arrived.

"My mind is officially off of work now."

He squeezes me against his body and I chuckle at the thoughts his Wolf is sending me.

"He's feeling pervy tonight," I remark.

"He wants you all to himself. He's not interested in game night."

I grin and run my hands over his chest some more, feeling the heat of his body burn through his shirt. "I get that, but it's just a little delay until we can get back to your place and then he can have his wicked way with me." I waggle my eyebrows as I say it and Tate barks out a laugh. I have a dirty burst of inspiration and blink coyly up at him.

"Did you notice if Pippa is still out front?" I ask him, my tone full of innocence.

"She was closing up the front desk when I came in, she mentioned something about checking in the books that had been returned in the back room."

I bite my lower lip and slide out of his arms, putting a little sway in my hips as I walk to the door. I turn around so I can watch him and maintain eye contact while I lock the door to my office.

"I like where you're going with this." He growls. I can see his Wolf flash in his eyes and heat swirls down to my core. My legs feel hot and my nipples get tight.

"We'll have to be very quiet," I whisper. His gaze travels over my body. I can feel his eyes as they travel over me. His breath hitches as he watches me slowly curl the fabric of my dress up my thighs. I'd taken my panties off about an hour ago, in the hopes of surprising him and also saving my favorite pair. I walk the fabric higher up my legs until I feel the air cool against my flushed center and we're both panting with need. Tate's Wolf is nearly howling his approval into my mind and I tremble with anticipation. The idea that we might get caught has added an unexpected thrill to what's already scorching hot between us. His eyes are nearly black pools of hunger and I realize he likes the danger of potentially getting caught too.

"Can you be quiet?" I breathe. I smile as he slowly stalks over to me, literally a wolf on the hunt. His footsteps are silent. My pulse flutters in my throat and prickles of awareness skate over my skin. He stops right in front of me, his big body crowding mine but I don't feel threatened. Oh no, I feel revered, adored, utterly safe. His chest is practically heaving and the heat of his body pushes against me. He silently drops to his knees and pushes his face into my ribs. He rubs his scratchy stubble against my dress and breathes deeply. I love it when he does this, it's like a cat scent marking, but so unbelievably sexy. I feel his hands slide up my bare legs and he stills when his fingers brush the curve of my bum and finds nothing there. He growls, soft and low in his throat. The sound sends a spike of desire down to my belly and I squirm a little against the door.

"Can you?" He breathes up at me.

34

Tate

What the ever-loving fuck have I done in my life to deserve this Goddess as my Mate?? She's pinned against the door of her office, my large body hemming her in, her arousal fucking perfuming the air, making my Wolf lose his Godsdamned mind. Dropping to my knees in front of her is my only option. She deserves to be worshiped and I'm a man possessed with a sudden and fierce piety.

I hold eye contact with her as I run my hands across her hips, around to her gloriously soft ass, and push my face against her belly. She trembles as I rub my face into her dress and work my hands around to lift first one leg, then the other over my shoulders. I bunch her dress in my hands and then over my head until I'm completely hidden under her skirt, the magic of her hot pussy making me delirious. I dive right in and lick a long line up the seam of her cunt, making her squeak above me.

"Quiet, Love." She moans so softly I can only hear her because of my Wolf, who is blisteringly happy right now. I can't stop the rumbling growl of pleasure that hums from my chest and I dip my mouth back against her pussy and feast on her. She holds onto my head, still wrapped up in her dress and she pushes her mound closer to me, rocking her hips, chasing her pleasure against my face and I fucking love it. I hold her hips tight, keeping her pinned against the door of her office and revel in her. I lick and suck along the side of her clit, the way I know she loves, and her whole body clenches with her orgasm. I keep licking her slowly, holding her against my mouth as she slowly comes down, gasping. I gently nip her inner thigh before I pull away, emerging from her skirts to watch her eyes as I lean back and unzip my jeans. Her cheeks and chest are beautifully flushed and her lips part as I pull my cock out. I'm as hard as steel for her and I stroke myself slowly. Her eyes flare even darker with her desire and I nearly groan out loud.

I raise my eyebrow and send her an image through my Wolf. We've never tried to communicate directly like this before but she gets the idea. She's still holding her dress up around her hips and I can see her glistening pussy as she steps over to me and sinks down onto my lap. I hold her gaze and fist my throbbing dick with one hand and guide the tip to her entrance. She's trembling and I shift my body so I can hold her up, my hands palming her luscious ass, spreading her open for me. She sinks down, down, down onto my dick until she's taking all of me. Her arms wrap around my neck and I rock my hips up into her. She leans into me and I kiss her, deep and wet. I swallow every sexy sound she makes while we grind our hips together slowly. I drive my cock as deep as she can take me. I squeeze her ass against me and hold her tight so the friction of our bodies rocking together rubs against her clit. She whimpers into my mouth and I increase my pace, but keep the pressure. I feel her cunt clench around me as she stiffens and her orgasm sweeps over her. My climax is not far behind and I shudder into her. Her hands are on my face and our mouths are pressed together and we just breathe, raggedly, against each other's lips. Her dark eyes are soft and full of wonder as she comes down from her second climax. I rock my hips against her slowly, just to make her feel good and her face transforms as she smiles openly at me.

"Well done you. My legs feel like jelly." She whispers, and then kisses my nose. I chuckle and pull my legs under me while I hold her against my hips and stand, keeping her speared with my cock. She squeals and throws her head back at the sensation and I turn us around so I can sit her down on the edge of her desk. I pull out of her, tuck myself back into my jeans and grab the box of tissues off the shelf next to her desk. I clean her up while she watches me with tenderness and affection, my Wolf pleased to be taking care of her.

"I think we can make it through game night now," I say, and she chuckles.

"We should be good for at least one campaign. Let's go save the world."

Desi has the board set up on the picnic table in their little courtyard. The patio lights are lit and a tray of snacks from the bakery is all set up next to a couple pitchers of lemongrass tea. As soon as Ulla sits down after hugging Desi, that bloody raccoon ambles over and pats her on the knee. I watch her as she scratches it behind the ears like it's a puppy and she filches one of Sela's cookies from the tray and gives it to the animal.

"Those are for humans, Ulla Mine." I mock growl at her. She just rolls her eyes at me and pets the little trash panda while it gets crumbs all over its grubby paws.

"Well, if that's the case, I guess we can't eat any either." She smoothly retorts.

"Touchè, I concede. Now save some of those for me." I sit down next to her and the raccoon eyes me warily. I keep my Wolf tucked down deep inside me. He's so satisfied from our romp in Ulla's office that he's not concerned about swinging our dick around to prove that we're higher in the pack than the little fuzzy gremlin eating my favorite cookies. I tip my chin at it and it scampers off, trailing crumbs.

"She's just hungry, her mama left her behind because she's got a funny back leg."

Well, now I feel like an asshole. Ulla smiles at me and bumps my arm with her shoulder.

"I sent her to my folk's place, Dad'll set her up in the tree fort since we all know Dennis is never going to use it."

I marvel at her kindness, even though it's not at all unexpected at this point. Desi straightens the last pile of cards with a flourish over to our right and swirls over to perch on the edge of the snack table.

"Dennis and the furball will get along just fine. Your mom'll be pissed though," She says lightly, wiggling her eyebrows conspiratorially. Ulla laughs and shrugs.

"At this point, she has to put on a good show just to maintain appearances. Raccoons aren't on the list, so Linda has a solid chance to sneak in there and charm her."

"Do all of the animals you talk to have middle management names?" I ask her, smiling. She beams back at me and shrugs.

"I don't name them, they just tell me."

"That raccoon told you that her name is Linda??" Suspicion is dawning on me.

"Not in so many words, but that's the gist of it." She

blinks her big eyes at me and I can feel her working me over.

"You're full of shit," I say. I cross my hands over my chest and lean back into the picnic table. Desi is chuckling quietly behind me, not bothering to hide that she's eavesdropping. I shoot her a glare and she laughs harder.

"I most certainly am not!" Ulla responds tartly. She sits up straighter, folding her hands in her lap. She looks prim and proper and fucking irresistible. She stares me down archly, her lips pursed adorably.

"I have a feeling you're naming these creatures ridiculous human names and they're too swayed by your charms to refute. If they even can. Do they speak English?? How does it even work?"

Behind me, Desi snorts.

"Careful there Sugar Cookie," She says quietly.

I'm unmoved. It started as a silly way to tease my girl, but now I'm genuinely curious.

"How do you understand your Wolf?" Ulla asks me in her quiet way.

I pause. I have to think about how to put it into words, and even when I do, it doesn't really explain anything.

"I just… do. His thoughts are my thoughts. His feelings are mine too. We're the same spirit, I think." I finish a little inadequately.

Ulla twists her mouth to the side in thought and I frown at my explanation. It's so much more than that, but I don't know if I can make anyone else understand it if they don't experience it for themselves. It's like when people say that you'll never understand parenthood until you have your own kids. You just can't know.

Just then Seb quietly steps into the courtyard and Ulla and Desi both jump up to help usher Cora in, who's carrying a box of what smells like Sela's cinnamon coffee cake and something with chocolate.

"Ooooh did you get the choco-bombs?" Ulla croons to her while simultaneously opening the box to see for herself. I grin as I watch her with her best friends, who are also my best friends, and I marvel again at how unbelievably fucking lucky I am. Deep contentment fills me as I soak up the family I've found for myself. Seb grunts next to me and we both just enjoy watching how happy our Mates are. Ulla's eyes are rolling back in her head while she eats some gooey, chocolate truffle thing and Desi and Cora are not far behind her in their own theatrics.

"They're going to eat everything," Seb mutters. I glance over at him, and he's just as moony as I am, stars in his eyes as he watches Cora wipe icing off her chin. The poor fucker. We're both tied to very different but perfect Mates and nothing can ruin my good mood tonight.

Ulla laughs at something Cora says under her breath and then she shivers.

"I'm going to run inside and grab my jacket, I think I left it here the other day," She says, separating herself from the snacks and rubbing her arms.

"You did Star Blossom, I put it on the hook in the back room," Desi says to her around a mouthful of cinnamon cake. She waves to Ulla to hop on in, and my lovely Mate sashays away from me. I enjoy the view of her round ass swaying and get a slap on the chest for it.

"Ow, what the fuck, Cora?"

"Don't ogle her. Jesus Christ, Tate, she's not an object for your enjoyment." Cora is glaring fiercely at me, but Desi is still just laughing around her cake.

"I know she's not an object, cool your jets Ace. But she has a very fine ass and I intend to enjoy looking at my

Mate. Are you telling me that you never watch Seb lift cords of wood around the shop?"

Her blush answers that question and Seb looks smug. Cora gapes at him with her mouth opening and closing like a little pink goldfish. Pinkfish? Whatever, it's cute as hell. She glowers at the both of us and practically stamps her foot.

"I'm freaking out a little bit you guys, I'm sorry I was shitty." She grouses. Seb lifts one of his tree trunk arms and she scuttles over to press herself into him. The mood shifts by several degrees of bummed-the-fuck-out as we all swing our eyes over to Desi.

"I haven't seen anything else Babes. All we're working with is what we've got. But it does seem to make sense that whatever's coming, is coming around the Solstice. It's the only thing I can think of that fits with the riddle." She shrugs, not meeting my gaze and looking chagrined. I suspect she knows more than she's letting on, but magic is tricky sometimes, and I know Desi would never willingly lead us astray, not when the stakes are so high.

We've been spending as much time as we can being sneaky assholes and trying to figure out what Desi's vision or premonition or whatever the fuck it was, means. Without actually telling Ulla about it. Desi still firmly believes that Ulla can't know, so she makes the choice she's meant to make. But it's practically giving me hives keeping a secret from her. It's also very hard since she can hear my Wolf in her head. I've done my best to keep my anxiety about all of this to myself, so I've been distracting her with a lot of sex. Like insatiable, porno-style sexy times. It's the only thing I can think of that'll keep our minds solely on each other and I'm not going to lie, it's not a hardship. My Wolf spends most of his energy on pleasing her, so he can't let anything slip. Now that she's been working days at the library, the rest of the gang and I have been racking our brains trying to figure out what might be coming. But so far we haven't come to any firm conclusions about anything other than the Solstice seems important.

Hold her close but not too tight,

The challenge is hers to make it right.

She'll make a choice when Moon and Mother lend her voice.

The balance shifts when the veil is thin, the shadow plots to be let in.

When the sun steals the sky from the moon,

The Green Man breaks the seal to force a boon.

We've been caught all over town by curious locals and we're starting to gain a reputation for being weird and in the way, spending most of our free time stalking and watching Ulla like extras from an espionage movie. And for a town that prides itself on being a little weird, that's saying something. Between the four of us, Ulla hasn't been alone for more than a few minutes in weeks. I'm not sure if what we're doing is helping at all, but we can't think of anything else to do to keep her safe. So she's shadowed by one of us at all times.

But none of us will give up, and none of us will let Ulla know that there's anything wrong. I don't love keeping things from her, in fact I fucking hate it. But if it will help keep her safe then I'll absolutely be a sneaky asshole.

My Wolf hears her footsteps and I grunt to the others to let them know. I give a tug on the Mate bond and send her a thread of devotion. She's smiling warmly when she steps out into the courtyard and heads straight for me. She slides her arms around my middle and I tuck my chin on the top of her head, nestling her in as close as I can get her. Her smaller body fits so perfectly next to mine and I soak her in. Willing her to be safe. But that thread of worry is now ever-present and I blink to push it down inside me as far as I can.

"Did Desi finish off the almond cookies before you got any?" She asks me, a smile in her voice. I grunt and squeeze her tighter.

"Why do you ask?"

"You seem a little sad, and I know how much you love those cookies."

I give my head a little shake and force a smile on my face.

"Nah babe, you're my favorite cookie now."

"Jesus fucking Christ, that's baaaaad." Cora groans, rolling her eyes at me. But Ulla just laughs, which was my intention, and the rest of us get into the game.

35

Ulla

I wake up on Saturday morning feeling itchy and restless. It's a new feeling for me. I slip out of Tate's bed and pad lightly to the kitchen to put on the kettle and grab a scone from the box in the freezer. We must have bought Sela out of all her baked goods the other day for game night, because we each managed to wrangle a full box of goodies home after we very satisfactorily wiped the board free of all mutations and what have you's. I enjoy game night as much as the rest of them, but my joy comes more from watching the rest of the crew dance around Cora and her intense competitive streak. We all love her and embrace her quirks, and her laser focus on dominating a board game is a sight to behold. She's just so prickly and the way she gets personally offended by the cards in the draw pile makes me smile and love her all the more.

I've been enjoying so much time with my friends, it feels as if they're never far from me lately, and after so long being away and solitary, it's a welcome change. Everything about being back in Eliza Falls feels good. Wonderful even. But all the time spent either cocooned with Tate or laughing with Desi and Cora means I haven't had a moment to myself in weeks. I'm looking forward to my Solstice ritual of hiking alone in McLaren this afternoon. I suspect I'm feeling a bit restless because I haven't had any solitude to let my mind settle in the last little while.

The kettle boils and I pour the water over my tea and move to the living room, snacks in hand. I hear scratching at the door and wander over to peek through the side window. I blink a couple of times and finally just accept that stranger things have happened and open the door.

A rather large chicken with an impressive wattle is standing on the back of a turtle. I can see another hen out in the yard, but she doesn't seem interested in me or the scene in front of me, so I look back to the odd couple and tilt my head.

"Do you guys need to come in? Is that something you do?" I ask them quietly. Tate was up late last night, generally being amazing and blowing my mind in the bedroom, and I'm planning to let him sleep in. I want to wake him up in my own way once he's slept long enough, but I have a feeling I won't be doing anything until I get rid of these two. The chicken scratches her little foot along the back of the turtle's shell and they both just stare at me. I feel their thoughts push at my awareness and open up that part of me… I've gotten into the habit of mentally pushing back the gift that lets me hear animals since things have gotten so weird since Tate and I completed the Mate bond. I don't know what the deal is yet, but after the bee incident, I've started practicing mentally closing that door so we can enjoy each other without an audience. I shudder to think about that day in the little copse behind my parent's backyard.

I let my eyes get unfocused and think about the latch I put on the mental door inside my head. It's a simple visualization that works for a lot of people, and I'm getting better each time I try it. I unlock the door and let it swing open. The rushing sound of all of the living things around me swirls through my mind and I close my eyes to concentrate on the two closest to me. The hen and the turtle's thoughts are a bright yellow ribbon and I let it float up to me.

I blink my eyes open, the surrounding tree voices a rustling hush all around me, like waves crashing in the distance. There's a chiming sound of some other wild animals in the woods behind Aunt Jett's home, raccoons I think, and the tinkling voice of the Falls, ever present in the background of everything. Her voice is gentle and sweet, even though her currents are fast and strong. Her voice has become a welcome white noise I lean into whenever the brighter voices of the other wildlife become too insistent.

"Oh," I whisper. "Um, I don't think that's the best idea."

The chicken tilts her head and taps the turtle's shell with her scaly little foot, then makes a shockingly loud dinosaur sound. I blink in surprise.

"Absolutely not!" I hiss.

She stamps her other foot and clucks mulishly. I hold my ground, crossing my arms over my chest and frowning. After a stare down of what feels like many minutes, she finally tosses her head and blinks her beady eyes at me, with what feels distinctly like disdain, and flutters off the back of the turtle. Who, in classic turtle fashion, slowly starts turning around.

"She's mean, you can do better Usain," I whisper at the turtle's back. I get the sense that he doesn't really care what I think, so I gently close the door.

I shriek when I turn around directly into Tate's big chest.

"Holy crap! I didn't hear you come up behind me!"

He grins his sweet grin and chuckles as he leans down to kiss my cheek. As he straightens back up, he pulls a bouquet of wildflowers from behind his back with a flourish worthy of a stage magician.

"Aww! These are beautiful, thank you." I take them and press the blossoms into my face.

"Wait, where did you even get these? You were asleep!"

"Ah, a magician never reveals his secrets." He wiggles his eyebrows at me and leans down again for another kiss, which I happily provide. Smiling at each other, we settle into the kitchenette and make tea and toast, enjoying a quiet morning ritual.

"Was that one of the chickens riding on Usain I saw on the deck?" He asks.

"Yep, I'm pretty sure it's The Duchess. She's mean." I huff.

Tate barks a laugh, nearly snorting his tea through his nose and carefully puts his mug down. "What?!"

"Ugh, don't ask. They scratched at the door while I thought you were sleeping. She wanted to come inside and go into the bedroom. When I said no, she was really salty about it!" I laugh at the absurdity of it and let my frustration go. While I can hear them, I've never been able to understand some animals, and this hen is one of them. Tate snorts again, and asks, "Why on earth did she want to go into the bedroom?"

"You don't want to know."

He laughs again and I soak in his good humor. He really is just a lovely person, his laughter deep and rich, making me feel like all's right with the world. How can things be bad when there are people like Tate around?

"I'm heading into the rescue center this morning to get the big dogs out for a run before lunch. What are your plans for the afternoon?" He asks, picking up his mug again.

"I want to take a walk through McLaren, it's a Solstice tradition for me to wiggle my toes in the woods and soak up some of the energy on the longest day. There's a little extra magic in the air during the Solstices and Equinoxes, and I like to honor the seasons in my own way."

His brow furrows a little and I tilt my head. He catches me looking at him and smoothes his expression. Curious. I feel a nudge through the bond from his Wolf and blush. He grins and arches an eyebrow.

"Shall I honor your seasons in my own way before you head out?"

Oh good grief. I bite my lip and slide out of my chair, putting extra sway into my hips as I walk around the little table to stand in front of him. I put a little purr into my voice as I lean down and push my cheek gently against his morning stubble.

"I can make some time in my busy weekend schedule for something, what do you have in mind?"

Images from his Wolf immediately flood my brain and I groan. My body responds immediately to his ideas, and Tate's hands slide up my bare legs as I watch his eyes flash with heat.

"Back to the bedroom, we'll need some room to maneuver."

36

Ulla

Walking through these woods has always settled me. Whatever it is inside that needs trees around me, is calmed the most when I'm out here. There's something extra in the air today though. This is the first time since I was a little girl that I've been able to get this deep into nature during the Solstice. My years living in the city had only really allowed me to go to the beach or take a busy hiking trail. It feels nice to know that I'm alone with my thoughts, or at least away from other people.

Mom and I used to make flower crowns every year and dance in the yard. Dad had brought home a little gas powered fire pit when I was eleven and it became one of our family traditions. I smile as I reach up and touch the crown I'd made myself earlier. The flowers Tate brought me this morning are so beautiful, I couldn't resist honoring the longest day by making them into a crown for myself.

Thinking about Tate floods my body with hot, hungry flames. We've been so wrapped up in each other lately. It feels so good to be with him. I feel my cheeks flush as I recall what we did this morning. Good gracious, that man plays my body like a desperate, horny fiddle. I can't get enough of him, and my heartbeat picks up as I think about our plans for tonight.

Smiling to myself, I let my mind wander as I slowly walk through the forest, not really paying attention to my surroundings. I can hear the Falls that give this wonderfully weird little town its name, roaring off in the distance. I'm farther into the woods than I usually let myself go. But it's such a quiet morning and the whispers of the trees around me are soothing. I don't fret when I'm alone in the forest. Maybe that's foolish, but I trust the voices of the creatures around me to alert me to anything dangerous before it becomes an issue. I've never felt afraid when I'm surrounded by nature, and I'm not about to start now.

I left my purse and shoes back in my car in the visitor lot and my bare feet on the soil connect me to the earth in a comforting and tangible way. I sigh as I run my fingers through the leaves in the low bushes all around me and listen to the bird calls in the surrounding trees.

I feel a rustling in the leaves around me, a skittering of awareness that raises the hairs on the back of my arms, but just as quickly, a sense of deep peace settles over me. I continue walking aimlessly, letting the wind carry me, breathing in the magic of this place. As I inhale the loamy scent of the underbrush, the air starts to feel heavy and a soft pressure makes my ears pop. I stop and frown. The sounds of the woods are strangely muted, and the air around me begins to take on a heaviness I've never encountered before. It's distinctly warmer now too. I stop where I am and stand quietly, listening to the voices of the trees around me, hoping to get a sense of what I'd inadvertently stepped into. The rushing sound of the Falls is now muted and the trees are utterly still.

Oh no.

This doesn't feel right. A sense of foreboding creeps along my skin and I look around me, although I'm not sure what I'm looking for. I really wish I'd told Tate exactly where I was planning to go this morning. Or had thought to keep my phone on me. I don't plan on needing rescuing, but if I'm attacked by a cougar or bear out here that I can't connect to, it would be nice to have my body found before the scavengers do their thing. Goosebumps spread out over my whole body and I shiver despite the muggy heat that now surrounds me. It feels like I'm in a little pocket of hot, stale air.

A twig snaps over to my left and I twirl around to see what's prowling around over there. What I see is so unexpected, all I can do is gape at it.

At him?

A tall, mostly naked man is walking toward me. His body is big and strong, with an impressive rack of antlers sweeping up from his brow. His gate is sure. He doesn't mince through the underbrush, placing his feet just so. Nope. This man walks with the confidence of a God. As soon as I think that, I realize who I'm looking at.

The Green Man is a Fae legend I've read about in my research. Often portrayed as a consort to the Goddess, he's a force of nature to be reckoned with. He's wild and untamed and he heralds the changing of the season and the return to Spring. I frown; I've never read about him walking abroad in the Summer... But magic is a wily mistress and mortals are foolish to assume anything when it comes to elemental magics.

I feel a tug in my chest that I can't quite place. Something is pulling at my awareness, but the creature in front of me is demanding all of my attention. I can't look away. His eyes are deep pools of inky black, all pupils and no iris. He's watching me with a slightly curious expression, like he's not sure if he likes what he's looking at. I don't like this. A sense of wrongness sweeps over me, but it's swept aside quickly, like it wasn't expecting me to notice it.

You are not what I expected, a deep booming voice suddenly speaks in my head.

Oh Godsdamnit, he's talking to me directly in my brain! This can't be good. I try to calm my racing heart, but he tilts his head sharply and all my efforts to chill the fuck out are thwarted.

You smell like Wolf, I am displeased.

Something ripples around him and I feel fear cascade down into my bones.

"Uh, sorry?" I reply, my voice trembling. My whole body is shaking now and it feels like my feet are rooted to the spot. As I think that, I realize that tendrils of morning glory have crept over my feet while the Green Man was staring at me and I shake myself. I take a deep breath in and send my awareness out into the vines and they slow their creep towards me. I don't like this at all. The Green Man frowns when the ivy retreats and he looks back to me.

Your gifts are vast, little one, the time has come for you to take your place.

Um, what?

37

Tate

I'm practically jaunty as I haul Daisy back towards the kennel yard. Our morning run was as refreshing as it usually is, and her big body bounces around me in doggy joy. She and I have been going out on weekly forest runs for the last year. Once I realized she wasn't getting all of her energy out in her daily walks with the other volunteers, I stepped in and took her out for proper *Runs*. Capital R. The first time I shifted with her she gave me the side eye. But once she got over her initial wariness of my Wolf shape she became enthusiastic. We run all over the woods behind the rescue center and once we wear her out, she'll happily nap the rest of the day away. Rain or shine we come out here once a week.

As I get Daisy settled back into her kennel, I think about Ulla and her midsummer forest rambling plans. She'd been chirping happily about her annual tradition to get outside on the Summer Solstice all week, and I smile to think about her walking through the trails like a barefoot Disney Princess. I pulled myself away from her this morning while she still slept, popping out to pick up a bouquet of blooming summer wildflowers to surprise her. The sight of her when I got back, still sleeping and tangled up in my dark green sheets, sent a thrill of pleasure through me, my Wolf utterly satisfied. Her delectable softness and her cloud of white hair, oh my Gods *her hair*, all wrapped up in my scent nearly dropped me to my knees. How did I get so lucky? What have I ever done to deserve this incredible Mate? I pretended to be asleep when she snuck out of bed a little later and listened to her pad around my apartment. She's so cute when she thinks no one's watching her and the shock that shot through the bond when Aunt Jett's hen bitched at her was adorable. Those chickens are ridiculous, and I love them.

My girl loved the flowers as I thought she might, and we enjoyed a sleepy morning cup of tea together, like an old married couple. It fills my heart with an indescribable joy to have these little moments with her. I smiled when she told me about her forest plans for the afternoon. Today is the Solstice and as much as the gang and I have been working to make sure she's safe, other than following her everywhere, we haven't come up with anything to really do. There are no signs pointing to anything at all, and I'm starting to wonder if maybe Desi's vision is wrong. Plus the woods are the safest place for her, her gifts being what they are.

When Ulla caught my frown at breakfast, I shoved my worries down deep and sent her some dirty fantasies through the link between us. Her arousal flooded my senses then and I'd shucked my clothes faster than a honeymooning virgin shucked oysters. I climbed back into bed with her and she'd moaned and writhed as I worshiped her properly. Cherishing her with my mouth on her cunt and my hands roaming all over her skin is my new favorite.

Her soft sounds of pleasure and the way she meets me

thrust for thrust only heighten my wonder at her. She's such a delicate seeming, quiet creature that her voracious need when we come together is a revelation. She's as fierce and demanding in bed as she is sweet and soft out of it. The dichotomy of her drives me bonkers, my Wolf desperate to get back to her as soon as possible. He's prowling inside me as I sign myself out of the volunteer logbook at the front desk and I nod to Mel as I walk out to my truck.

I only make it about halfway back to town when the hair on the back of my neck stands up and my Wolf suddenly starts growling deep. My phone rings, the sound jarring in the quiet cab of my truck, and I pull over to the shoulder and set the truck in park. I pull my phone out of my pocket and frown at Desi's contact picture.

"Hey," I start.

"Where's Ulla??" Desi demands.

Ice flows through my body faster than I can draw breath.

"She's taking a Solstice stroll through the woods, an annual tradition apparently. Why, Desi?" I say, my voice strained as I send a pulse of energy down the link of our mating bond. I can feel Ulla at the other end of it, but the bond feels off. Thick, like I'm pushing through sand, I can't quite grasp what I'm reaching for. My Wolf is prowling through my insides in a fury. His fear drives my own.

"Get to her now Tate, go to the Falls, she's walking into a trap."

The line goes dead and my heart stops in my chest. My Wolf is barely contained, his palpable despair the only thing I can feel. We'd been so careful to mind Desi's premonition. But over the last couple months of wooing Ulla, of making her ours and discovering nothing that pointed to a tangible threat, I'd let my guard down. Desi's voice comes back to me then, her voice so unlike her own.

When the sun steals the sky from the moon,

The Green Man breaks the seal to force a boon.

I throw myself out of the truck and into the woods as I let my Wolf out. We can track her better in Wolf form and nothing is going to stop me from reaching her. I only hope I get there in time.

38

Ulla

The creature's voice booms inside my head like thunder. So much of this doesn't make any sense. Least of all what he's saying.

"What do you mean, 'take my place'?" I ask him, my voice sounding small in the thick air.

The Earth demands her Queen returned, you have dallied here long enough.

Whaaat the fucking *what?*

I blink a few times and try to make this make sense. Perhaps I've hit my head? Maybe I fell into a ravine and I'm laying at the bottom, bleeding out and this is my mind's way of processing death? That would make more sense than me stepping into a fairy tale nightmare and being told that I need to return somewhere and… *wait.*

"Um, Sir. Ah, when you say that the 'Earth demands her Queen returned', what exactly do you mean by that?"

The black eyes staring at me narrow, and I shrink back a little bit.

Your games are unwelcome, I am sent to retrieve you and return you to Faerie.

Still not making sense.

"Because I am… what exactly?"

I feel the anger bristling off of him and it bites at my skin. The trees around us are beginning to rustle and I can feel the tension begin to swirl around me.

This is tiresome. Your power has only grown in your time here. Now the balance must be restored.

The frustration radiating off of him is thick and pushes against me.

Your time in the human world is over now.

"I just don't understand, I'm not the Queen of anything, and I'm certainly not going anywhere with you."

His skin ripples with energy as I watch him glare at me. I'm not sure who or what he thinks I am, but I don't care. The idea that I'm some sort of Fairy Princess is ludicrous! I'm a nerdy librarian with the mildest nature magic. I can talk to trees for crying out loud. That definitely doesn't make me Fae royalty.

"I think you have me confused with someone else," I say, slowly backing away from him. I send my thoughts out to the wilderness around me and try to pull energy into myself. It isn't something I've done a lot of, but I don't like the way this horned guy is looking at me. When I first saw him, he was regal and austere. Now that I've pissed him off and he's clearly struggling to hold his shit together, he's starting to blur around the edges.

Dread pools in my belly as I watch his form shift right in front of me.

Not good. This is seriously not good.

I don't know a lot about the Fae, but I'm pretty sure that something powerful enough to speak directly into my mind and also change forms isn't someone I want to have mad at me. Or noticing me at all. Oh Gods. I'm probably about to die. I should have had more sex with Tate.

My stomach drops as I reach inward to feel the bond between us and I can't hear him. Whatever magical bubble the Green Man is wielding is blocking our connection. It feels like screaming underwater, vague and blurry. The creature standing before me is no longer the Green Man that I recognize from myth. Gone is the proud guardian of rebirth and renewal. In his place is a monster straight out of a horror movie. His shoulders have rolled forward, his head tilting to the side and his once gleaming antlers are now black and dripping. Is that.. old blood?? He's also somehow even taller now? Ohmygods, this is so, so bad!

I wish to make this simple. You have only to accept your place.

"I don't have a place in Faerie!" I cry.

Your power comes from Faerie, therefore you are a worthy sacrifice.

Sacrifice?? Oh helllll no!

Panic surges through my body as I watch the creature in front of me continue to morph into a new terror. The light of the forest around me deepens and shifts, shadows creeping over the small clearing we're trapped in. His once elegant fingers are now curled and tipped with wicked claws. His hunched back has sprouted twiggy hair all across his shoulders and electricity sparks across them. He steps towards me and the ground trembles beneath him. I scrabble backward to maintain some distance. I have a sinking feeling that if he gets his horrifying hands on me that I'll be out of choices.

My chest pulls heavily and I gasp as I realize that I can hear Tate's Wolf suddenly.

"NO!" I shriek. "Stay away!"

My blood thunders in my ears and I feel the ground shuddering under my feet. Like a great stampede is heading this way. The monster in front of me quirks his head, listening to the sound of my Mate tearing up the underbrush to get to me. No! Oh Tate, *no*. My terror intensifies as I watch the creature in front of me smile maliciously as he too realizes what is coming.

This is an acceptable alternative. I will destroy this one and you will have no reason to linger here. The voice oozes in my mind. No! Nononononononono. Tate is too good, too kind. He'll think he's doing the right thing, the chivalrous, stupid, dangerous, helpful thing by fighting for me and probably dying for me Godsdamnit and I can *not* allow that to happen!

Tate blasts into the clearing, snarling and growling. His beautiful, golden Wolf shining like a beacon in the false night that surrounds us. He stops in front of me and faces the dark Fae. Who chuckles as if we've brought him a new toy.

39

Tate

Never have I run so hard or so fast. I can feel Ulla's confusion through the bond and it guides my steps through the forest. Usually when I'm in my Wolf form I can hear her voice in my head as if she's right next to me, her thoughts are a shining beacon. But something is interfering. I can sense her presence, but it's like listening to someone in another room.

I race past trees and rush through the underbrush, allowing nothing to slow me down. Following the bond towards her, I keep running, my heart pumping hard, fear driving me forward. Desi's voice whispers in my mind that it's a trap. I can't slow down but I have to be smart. If this is a trap then I can't fall into it. I push my legs harder, tearing up the forest floor under my paws. As I fly over a ridge covered in fern, the air around me suddenly pops like a bubble and I can hear Ulla in my mind again. Through Ulla's eyes, I can see the clearing she's in and hear the rushing of the Falls. I know where she is. I can see the creature she's facing and feel her fear.

"No! Stay away!" She screams. Her voice is full of

agony. Rage blisters through me and I snarl as I leap through a thicket of dense green and throw my bigger body in front of her small, precious form. I'll never let anything harm her.

Despair and frustration tumble down the bond between us and I can scent the tears running down her cheeks.

"Tate, *no!*" She cries and I realize too late she was telling me to stay away. I reach my thoughts through the link between us and feel her terror. She's afraid *for* me. She would have faced this strange monster on her own to protect me?! My fierce, brave Mate! I send her loving, proud thoughts and push my big body against her small frame. Electricity tingles where our bodies touch and she grabs fistfuls of my fur in her hands.

I will never leave you, Ulla Mine.

The creature chuckles an evil-sounding laugh as I push my body gently into Ulla, trying to put more space between her and danger. Her fists tighten in my fur, and I growl low towards him. His body is big, the antlers that sweep out from his head tall enough to tangle in the branches above him. Although I notice he isn't hampered by them at all. His skin is rough and craggy looking like he's made of tree bark.

Adrenaline is coursing through my body as I stare him down, my chest a constant rumble of aggression. In my Wolf form, I'm stronger, my wild nature at the front of everything. I have to force my thoughts to remain calm. I won't put Ulla in any more danger. But it's hard to hold my fury in check when I can feel her trembling behind me.

I can't keep my body still with all the aggression coursing through me, so I slowly stalk back and forth, keeping myself between Ulla and the creature. It's still chuckling in that sinister way and I feel Ulla stiffen behind me.

"You can't have him, he's MINE." She growls.

Can she hear him in her mind? Is he taunting her? I growl deep in my chest, and the creature shifts his gaze to me. There's clearly something going on here that I'm unaware of because my little Mate tries to get in front of me. I slink my body around her, maintaining myself as a shield.

I can hear her shouting at me through the bond, her voice terrified but sure. She doesn't want me in front of her. My human mind can understand that she might have a plan, but I'm too much in my Wolf right now and he can't let her get any closer to the monster in front of us. It's shifted even more since I burst into the clearing, its shoulders rolling forward and sharp, twiggy spikes growing out of its hunched back. Ulla's fear intensifies and I crouch. Just in time to snarl as the creature lunges for me.

Ulla's fear in my mind spurs me on as I begin to grapple with the monster, its long black claws sweeping through the air to slash my throat. I tumble away from Ulla, taking the fight away from her, snapping at the legs of the now lumbering Fae nightmare and feeling the passage of its claws pass through my long ruff. Ulla is sending love and pride through the bond, desperately trying to support me but not get underfoot. I'm whirling back at the Fae, its breath rancid and hot, its long arms swinging around to catch me. But I'm too fast, my Wolf a blur of motion, and I catch the monster's shoulder instead. I thrash my head around to inflict maximum damage. It howls, a sound full of rage and disbelief.

But quickly, I'm on the defensive as it extends the spikes growing out of its back even longer, and I have to let go before they lodge in my muzzle.

I dance back, snarling, and the Fae is no longer laughing. Black blood oozes out of its shoulder like oil, and it drags that arm across the ground like it can't lift it any higher. I don't trust it to not be a trick, so I circle wide, keeping it away from Ulla and keeping myself out of its reach. I can feel her behind me, her light through the bond clear and bright. She's still terrified and that stokes my fury. A Mate should never be afraid, they should always be safe and protected. Her fear is quickly replaced with frustration.

"Stop chastising yourself! This hardly counts as ORDI-NARY!" Ulla cries out. I stand taller and roar at the Fae. This needs to end. The Fae has been slowly creeping towards Ulla while we've been circling each other and I catch movement out of the corner of my eye. Ulla shrieks suddenly and I feel roots tangle under my feet. I jump to avoid getting caught but I've walked right into the Fae's plan. He charges at me, swinging that arm he's been dragging, now fully healed and glistening with his black blood. I twist in midair and close my jaw onto the Fae's neck, but it's too late. As I tear into his craggy skin with my teeth, his deadly claws rip into my belly. Searing heat and the precursory idea of pain shoot into my spine and all over my body. A tearing release of pressure in my guts as the Fae pulls his claws away tells me bad things. Very bad things. Darkness swarms my vision and I struggle to stay upright, refusing to leave Ulla defenseless, but it's too much. I can feel my intestines pushing at the edges of my skin and I stumble to the ground. I try to look back for my Mate, but the tearing in my core won't let me move. All I can hear is a high-pitched whine, until I hear nothing at all.

40

Ulla

I watch, frozen in horror as Tate stumbles and crashes to the ground. The gash in his side is oozing dark blood and *Oh Gods*, I can see his insides! The cackles of the dark Fae ring out around me, pinging off the trees. I break out of my shocked stillness and race to Tate's side. His breathing is shallow and ragged. The wet sound of bubbling as he inhales shoots ice through my veins. Oh no oh no oh *noooonooonooo*. My hands flutter helplessly over him, I'm afraid to touch him in case I cause him any more pain and helpless tears fall down my cheeks and drip off my chin.

You are both foolish children, the horrible Fae's voice barrels through my mind.

Nothing on this plane is powerful enough to thwart me. I will take you both back to Faerie and consume your bond. I will become the most powerful Lord the Ancestors have ever known and all will bow before my feet.

"Are you fucking *monologuing* right now?" I shout my incredulity. My body begins to thrum with rage and despair. I'm done being afraid. I gently place my hands on

Tate's side, my beautiful Mate going still under my hands. Avoiding the worst of his injuries, I send a pulse of energy into him. The response is a soft whine and a zing of electricity back up through the bond. He's still in there, we're still connected. And I've had *enough of this*! All the fear and helplessness and impudent rage that's been coursing through me since this started begins to boil up inside me. I allow my fury to wash over me. I rise to my feet and glare at the dark Fae. He's smug in his victory. I can sense that he believes in his megalomania.

Not today motherfucker.

A horrible calm flows over my mind and body, a terrifying *knowing* filling my senses as I realize what I can do. I close my eyes and picture the door I keep in my mind. The lock is shiny and strong, the wood polished and well-loved. This is not a doorway to a room I want to avoid anymore. This is a portal to a part of me that I was unsure of, a part of me that felt a little too wild, so I gently closed the door to deal with it later. But the swirling voices on the other side of that door are my allies. I can feel their encouragement as I unlock the latch. Bright, blinding light is seeping around the cracks of the frame, and I swing the door open wide.

All the voices that have been tapping at the edges of my awareness rush over me and I let them sink into my mind, feel them flow into my body. They fill me up with light and love and I invite them in deeper. The power swirling inside me is bright and hot and so, so alive. I send the magic dancing into every part of me. Soon it feels like my own edges are blurring and I send the twined magics out into the woods. Like spilling water across a countertop, my power flows over everything it touches and I call to every living thing around me. Every tree, every blade of grass, every bird, animal and insect. I send my power over them and I ask for their help. I lovingly demand it. I show them what we're fighting for and I push my need, hope and love into all of the life surrounding us. And they respond in kind. Hot, golden energy begins to flow back towards me and as it combines with itself and coalesces, it becomes a tsunami of undiluted *life*. It crashes into my body and I spin it in my mind like Rapunzel spins her thread. More and more of it spools inside of me until my fingertips feel hot and I'm vibrating with the power of it all. Never before have I pulled this much into myself. It feels like I'm overflowing, like the heat of a fire breaking over a crest, a great vortex of energy spinning inside of me.

My eyes are still closed as I separate a thread and send it down the bond to Tate. I carefully push the heat and light and love into Tate's still body to force the dark Fae's black magic out of him. He shudders and I feel the moment his blood no longer runs black and thick. The evil is forced out and his wound is now flushing out bright red blood in its place. I use the thread I've sent down the bond to stitch up the torn flesh and close the horrible wound. I kneel next to him and put my hand on his flank. I feel my hands get hot and I push a little more magic into him to make sure he'll survive. I can feel his heart beating steady and strong. I send a request out to the woods to protect him and sense a rustling all around us. I stand and open my eyes. The Dark Fae is still standing in the clearing, the foolish creature not realizing yet that I'm taking control of this. I glance down and see the underbrush slowly surrounding Tate and gently covering him. My Wolf is pulled under and away, vines of ivy curling around him, protecting him while he sleeps.

The Fae looks at me then and I smile, and I can feel how feral it is. His expression falters as he finally notices the change in the air.

What have you done?

I don't answer him with words. I reach my power out farther, pulling in more and more pulsing, green-gold energy. It fills me to the brim and shimmers at the edges of my body. My fingers tingling, my eyes shining and my hair standing on end. All of my terror and rage have boiled down to a burning, hot ball of light that I form in my hand. The Fae looks surprised.

You cannot be! You have been gone for too long. Your magic should be broken. This is not possible.

I look hard into his solid black eyes and flex my fingers. The power in my palm pulses, the heat of it traveling up my arm.

"You will never harm anyone, ever again," I say. My voice is different, deeper somehow. Like it's my voice layered over itself a hundred times over. The Fae steps back and stumbles. His broken horns catch in the branches around him, branches that weren't there before. He's been slowly surrounded by a copse of birch, hemming him in. The land is working against him at my request.

I close my eyes but can still see. The outline of everything around me is clear and bright, sparkling energy tracing through every living thing. I lift my fist and send the light into him. Like a canon, the magic explodes out of my palm, a volley of unadulterated life, searing hot and so bright it rivals the sun. It hits his chest and sinks inside of him with a crash that sends him to his knees. His eyes grow wild and frantic as he scratches and tears at his own flesh.

No! This cannot be!

His voice cries out inside my head, but it's not as loud as the life energy of the earth that still thrums through me. I feel my magic humming throughout my body, pushing at all of my edges. I watch as the Fae begins to shake, and cracks appear all over his body, the hot light of power I sent into him looking for a way out. Bright, pulsing energy forces the cracks all over him to expand, and his screams shake the leaves around us. Tender green tendrils of new growth spill out of the cracks, racing over the creature as it struggles.

I send a thought into the clay beneath my feet and watch as the ground underneath him crumbles and begins to consume him. Like a mudslide in reverse, the earth climbs up his thrashing body and begins to pull him down. Back into the land. The light inside of him burns even brighter as he's completely submerged into the ground. The vines consuming him spread across the ground and wind up the trunks of the birch trees standing sentinel. A great rumbling tremor shakes the earth, and then he's gone.

I kneel and put my hands to the place where he was just a moment ago and search for him. There's no sign he was ever here. I let the weight of everything bow my shoulders forward. The trembling begins in my hands and quickly spreads to my whole body. The power pulsing inside me needs to be released and I take a deep breath in.

As I exhale, I let it all go. The golden light flows out of me like my power did earlier, pouring over everything it touches. Sinking back into the trees and animals and earth. I send my gratitude out with it, thanking every creature and life for their aid.

As the power leaves my body, a chill sweeps over me and I fall back into the moss that has crept all around me. The soft, green bed pillows my fall as everything in my vision swims and grows dark.

41

Ulla

I t's warm.

I feel softness and warmth all around me. The light is a fluttering, deep pink and I let myself soak in the peace I'm floating in.

Wait.

Am I dead?

A soft, feminine chuckle rings out just to my side and I blink my eyes open and look around. I'm in a bright, flower-filled clearing, soft moss under my cheek. I hear birds chirping and when I look to my left I see a family of deer calmly grazing nearby. The sky is a bright, clear blue and I'm looking out at unfamiliar mountains.

There's a real *Sound of Music* vibe to the whole scene and I look over to where I heard the soft laughter and I squeeze my eyes shut again.

"You are not dead, my Daughter." Her voice sounds like bells and angels and birthday cake. I feel her amusement flow over me like a caress and open my eyes to look at her again. Her skin is a rich, gleaming, dark brown like the earth and her hair is a nimbus of white waves. She has slanted, bright green eyes and long, soft limbs adorned with flowers. There are flowers all over her. They adorn her flowing dress and drape across her shoulders like a cape, both seemingly colorless and yet every color at once. Her features are a little angular, her nose sharp like her gaze. I look into her hair and yep, I knew it, she's got pointy elf ears. I exhale a groan as I sit up and shake my head.

"Are you sure I'm not dead? This is pretty much my idea of what heaven would look like."

She smiles serenely at me.

"This place will be what you need it to be."

Huh. I look around and blink through the glitter in my eyes. It feels like the air is waiting for me to decide.

"What is it really?" I ask her. I feel cocooned in peace. I'm not mad about it. Maybe I couldn't be even if I wanted to? That makes me frown. The woman smiles brighter at me then, flashing dainty fangs.

"You are wise Little Daughter. This is a Between place. The magic here encourages peace. I am pleased that you noticed so quickly."

I press my lips together.

"Am I your child?" I ask her softly.

"Yes," She says, warmth in her voice. "But not in the way you ask. All living things are my children."

Oh.

"Um, are you mad that I killed the dark Fae who attacked me?"

"No Little One, I am not angry with you. He has lived his time and now he is at peace within me again."

Huh. Okay then.

"Do I have to stay here in the Between place?" I ask her.

She settles herself more comfortably on the moss next

to me and I wonder at that. Is she sitting like a human would to make me more comfortable?

"You ask good questions." She intones sagely. I blink and realize she heard the question I asked myself in my head. I'm going to have such a headache after today. She chuckles softly.

"I am not often around mortals, I find I am out of practice with waiting for your questions to spill out into the air." She nods deeply, like an apology. And I remember enough from what I've read, to understand that she won't say she's sorry. The Fae have rules around debts and I try to keep that in mind.

"You must choose, Little One. The Between place connects to the other realms. Your own included. There are many places a clever Wolf cub could thrive if you so choose." I blink at that. My mind flies to Tate and I shoot up.

"Oh my goodness! Tate! Is he alright?" I remember pushing as much magic as I dared into him, into his beautiful Wolf. He was so still. I remember his blood running clear and the ivy pulling him away from the Fae. I wring my hands and tremble where I stand.

"It appears that your choice is clear." She chuckles again, her sweet voice sounds like a song. "Yes, your Mate is safe and well. He still sleeps after your magic healed his grave wounds. I regret the actions of my oldest son. He has spent many centuries twisting his thoughts."

Wait.

Whoa whoa whoa.

"Your oldest son?" I gasp. As I understand it, Fae grow in power the older they are. If he was so old, he would have been incredibly powerful!

"How can I have defeated him? I'm just an Earth witch!"

"Ah my Little Daughter, you are much, much more than an Earth witch. You share some of their gifts, but you Dearest, are a powerful Fae."

Dark spots begin to dance at the edges of my vision and I flop back down onto my back. Breathing as slowly as I can manage, I turn my head to look at the woman again. She's watching me patiently, like a mother waiting for their child to realize their own potential.

"I am?" I breathe. I hear my blood rushing in my ears, and swallow hard.

"But I can just hear trees and animals sometimes… I thought…"

"Your magic has been suppressed in the human realm, it was believed making you appear more human would aid you there. But the Mate bond you share with the golden Wolf has opened the lines to your true self. Have you not noticed your gifts come to you more easily since you accepted the Bond?"

I think about that while I continue to manage my frantic heartbeat. I've been so wrapped up in my feelings for Tate that perhaps I've ignored the little things that had been calling for my attention. But thinking about it now, I visualize a few times when my gifts have felt more intense. This also explains the sex peepers. I press my lips together and cringe a little.

The beautiful woman laughs and nods sagely.

"Yes, Daughter, that is an effect of your full magic. You will be able to control that better with practice." Her smile is warm and a little knowing, like she and I share a secret. I bite my lip and feel my cheeks warm with mild embar-rassment.

"Ah, there is no need to feel that way. Coupling with your Mate is a sacred offering to me, and there is no shame to be had."

I feel myself blush even more and she laughs again.

"Can I ask you another question?" I say, mostly to change the subject, but also because this is something that's been bugging me since I woke up here. She nods her head and I take a deep breath.

"The scary Fae, he said that 'the Earth demanded her Queen returned'… Was that a trick?"

She holds my gaze with her bright green one, her eyes clear and unblinking.

"Would it change your choice if it wasn't?" She asks.

I think about it. If I accept that I'm some sort of Faerie Queen would I choose to stay here or go to some other realm where I can rule?

"Would it harm anything if it didn't?"

The goddess's eyes crinkle at the corners, her smile is so bright and wide.

"You would make an excellent Queen, Little Daughter. You ask very good questions. But no, no harm will come to Faerie if you choose to return to your Mate and the life you know. The realms are back in balance, and the remaining doorways between them are well hidden."

I close my eyes and lace my fingers together. I try to give the idea of never returning to Eliza Falls again and starting a new life as royalty in Faerieland a chance. I don't imagine it's all sunshine and roses since the Fae that attacked me was so utterly terrifying. I expect he's not the only one who is more nightmare than dream. I imagine the responsibility of choosing that path would be lifelong, and rewarding even so. But my mind and my heart keep turning back to Tate and my family. Cora and Desi and even Seb have become so precious to me. After a lifetime of being an outsider, they've opened their arms to me and I feel like I've found home with them. With Tate.

Something the Goddess said pushes at my thoughts

and I open my eyes. She's still watching me with her clear gaze, no pressure or expectation in her posture.

"I have made my choice."

She bows her head slightly to me, and I bow back to her.

"I wish to go back to my Mate and my life. But I have another question."

"Of course Little One, your mind is full of them, I am pleased to answer one more for you."

"You said before that the doorways between the realms are well hidden. How did I go through? I remember my life as a child, there are pictures of me with my parents as a newborn baby."

Her smile is serene, but there's a hint of sadness in her eyes as she replies.

"You were born to a princess of the Fae, during a time of unrest. You met my oldest son in your realm and saw how his heart was twisted into something dark. There are others who share his views and they work to overthrow the order of nature for their own gains. Your birth mother was a powerful Seer, and she had a vision of the war that was coming. She and your father, a guard in her service, were a love match, True Mates like you and your Wolf. Therefore, your birth was anticipated with joy. But he was slain in an insurrection and her heart was broken. She used the last of her gifts to send you through to the world you know, so that you might have a chance at a peaceful life. Love is the magic that created you and it is also the force that guides you. Your gifts are many, Little Daughter, and I have watched you grow into a wise and thoughtful woman. I am proud of you. Your birth parents would be too, had they the pleasure of knowing you. Never doubt that you are loved, for you are the Daughter of True Mates twice over."

I blink the tears out of my eyes, feeling them run down

my cheeks. A sad sort of calm settles over my shoulders, a quiet recognition of the loss of a family I never knew. But whose love and bravery allowed me to have the family I grew up with and the love that I know.

"I feel a lot of gratitude and acceptance for knowing this part of my story."

She smiles at me again, a crooked half-smile that's both rueful and pleased. I almost thanked her for telling me all of this, but remembered my research. My thanking her would have been viewed as magical capital, something that I would owe her in the future. By communicating my gratitude as my feelings, I'm able to sidestep the binding of that debt to her, and she's pleased with me.

"A powerful and wise Queen you would indeed be, but I respect your choice. "

"I won't forget your kindness," I reply. She leans forward and kisses my forehead.

"Go home to your Mate, brave Daughter."

I suddenly feel exhausted, sleep pulling hard at the edges of my mind. I blink at the vision of the Goddess in front of me and watch the edges of my sight grow dark. I slip back onto the soft moss, the warmth of this strange and beautiful mountain clearing sinking into my bones. Then soothing darkness sweeps over me and I sleep.

42

Tate

I wake up slowly.

I hear birds and the breeze through the trees above me. I feel the cool ground beneath my Wolf's body and a soft, warm presence at my side. I scent the air and it's all the expected scents of the woods around me, with the taste of the water from the Falls on the back of my tongue.

This is nice.

But why am I waking up in the woods? There's a nagging thought in the back of my mind, but I can't quite place it. I blink my eyes open, careful not to shift my big body. I feel a little stiff, but it's the weirdest thing, I don't remember why. It feels like I've been asleep for a long time. I realize slowly that the warm body curled up next to me is Ulla. I swing my head around to nuzzle her with my nose and she grumbles adorably in her sleep. I send a pulse down the bond and she's there, bright and clear and safe. Did we come out here for a run and decide to take a nap?

This is weird. But her breathing is low and slow, like she's deep in a dream and I'm loath to wake her. I curl my shaggy body around her smaller one and rest my head close to hers. I still feel really tired, so maybe just a little more sleep won't hurt. My Wolf will wake me if anything gets close to us.

I wake up again with a start. Footsteps are heading towards us and I smell sugar.

What the…?

I blink my eyes open and curl myself tighter around Ulla, who's still sound asleep tucked in next to me. The footsteps are getting closer and I can also hear humming now.

Ah. Desi.

Flashes of memory are starting to float back into my mind. I vaguely remember racing through the woods to protect my Mate, who I found facing a terrifying nightmare creature. I remember her fear and anguish when I charged into the clearing to stand between her and the monster. She was so scared but she stood her ground, and she'd shouted for me to get away, like she was trying to protect me. The memories flooding my mind are like a montage, the fight between the dark Fae and myself was brutal and embarrassingly short. I flinch as I remember the Fae slashing my belly and falling to the ground. Jesus christ, what the hell happened after I fell?

Desi's husky voice continues to sing slightly off key in her ridiculous way and I nudge at Ulla to wake her up. But she doesn't stir, she just keeps sleeping soundly.

"I'm nearly there my dearest Dumplings, make sure you're decent!" Desi singsongs loudly just over the nearest copse of birch. Wait. I don't remember those being here before. I run these woods regularly and all of the birches are closer to the South end of the park. I chuff low at Desi so she can hear where we are and her footsteps shift a little and head closer to us. She steps through a parting in the ferns and she smiles down at Ulla curled up tightly to my side.

"There she is, our very own Buffy the demon slayer."

Desi has a backpack over her shoulders, that she swings off and drops at her feet.

"There's a change of clothes for you and some protein bars and cookies in there. Seb sent along the jerky you like and there are two water bottles with electrolytes ready to chug. Our girl won't be waking up for a little bit so get yourself changed so you can carry her back to your truck. You left it running on the side of the road, but Seb ran over there and I've got your keys." She says, then spins around and drops to the ground. She sits cross-legged facing away from us and waves one hand in the air.

I growl low, not entirely sure why I'm feeling defensive, but I slip my big body away from Ulla and shift quickly. My abs are on fire as I stand up tall and stretch myself out. How long have I been asleep??

"You've been out cold since Saturday afternoon, SweetCheeks. It's Monday morning." Desi says softly.

I frown and blink at her.

"What the fuck?" I pull the boxer briefs out of the bag and slip them on. I'm startled to discover that I have a long, jagged scar running low across my belly, shiny and pink. I touch it gingerly and it's only a little tender.

"What happened Desi? I remember racing to save her, fighting a nightmare creature that was taunting her, and then… nothing."

She spins around and watches me slip on old jeans and a soft henley shirt that smells like Seb.

"Our girl stepped into her potential and destroyed that Fae asshole, that's what," Desi says, her voice full of pride. She looks down at Ulla, still sleeping curled up on the moss, and her gaze softens.

"She chose us over a life as a Queen, and she saved Faerie in the process."

"What are you even talking about Des, that creature was a huge monster that wiped the floor with me… how did she beat it? And a life as a Queen??" I stare at my Mate in wonder. She's so soft and small. Her breath hitches softly as we watch her and she burrows her little nose tighter into the ball she's made herself into. She doesn't look strong enough to open a new jar of pickles, let alone fight off a Peter Jackson nightmare.

Desi smiles ruefully and tilts her head to the side.

"Ulla might be the strongest of all of us, don't let her little package fool you."

I blink and then frown at Desi.

"What?"

Desi sighs, and I notice with a start that she's trembling. I watch her eyes fill with tears and for the first time since I've known her, she looks unsure.

"I couldn't say anything that might change her choice, but I was so scared Tate," She whispers. She wraps her arms around herself and her whole body shivers. I take a step toward her, but she holds a hand up to stop me.

"No, it's ok, I was mostly sure of her choice and that you'd be ok, but it wasn't *certain*. There were choices that would have changed everything and I just couldn't see until they were right on top of us. Things could have gone another way, and I was so afraid that I'd be burying you instead of talking to you right now. I like you a lot Beef Dip, and that really would've harshed my mellow." Her expression is rueful, but she's still pale. Ice skates down my spine as I realize how close we walked the line. If Desi was scared, then things were really bad. I've never seen her worried about anything, and I realize that I've come to take that for granted. I look at my dearest friend as she visibly shores herself up, wiping her cheeks free of her tears.

"I'm sorry Des, I had no idea this has been so hard for you. I was so wrapped up in my own shit, I didn't even consider how anyone else was dealing with things."

"That's how it's supposed to be! All the Faerie princess drama and talking to Goddesses stuff is where things got messy."

"Talking to Goddesses??" I ask her, incredulous.

"Keep up Honey Cruller."

I snarl at her and she laughs.

"Oh relax, our Girl will fill you in when she wakes up later." Desi is not swayed by my snarling and pulls out one of those foil emergency blankets from the backpack at her feet.

"Get your boots on, Paul Bunyan, scoop up your Mate, and let's go home."

43

Ulla

I'm so warm. Wherever I am, it's really soft and cozy, and it smells really good. Like the first day of summer and a good cuppa all rolled into one. First day of summer...

Something about that tickles the back of my mind, but I'm too cozy to wake up enough to really think about it. It's like a mosquito in the room, it's annoying, but hard to catch. I groan a little sigh of contentment and feel hot hands slide over my hips and pull me against a big, hard body. Mmmm, we're both naked. Oooh yes please, this is *very* nice. Tate's masculine chuckle ruffles the hair behind my ear and I smile in my sleep.

"You aren't sleeping, Love, I can hear you in my head," He says softly. His wonderful voice is so soothing and sends a thrill straight to my heart.

Wait.

"Tate!!" I shriek, scrambling around to face him. I blink the last of the sleep from my eyes as I take him in, scanning all of him that I can see. He looks ok. Better than ok! His color is good and his eyes are bright. I push him back and climb on top of him and move the sheets and blanket away from his chest and down to his hips.

"Slow down there Tiger, you've been asleep for a while, let's feed you before we get frisky," He says, his beautiful face alive and smiling. I push the bedding away from his belly and run my hands over his new scar. It's pink and shiny but it's healed up beautifully.

I burst into tears. Big, sobbing, blubbering tears that roll down my cheeks and shake my body.

"Oh Love, it's ok." He says. He sits up and wraps his arms around me while I let go of the fear and cry everything out all over him. I scootch in as close to him as I can and burrow into his chest. He holds me tight and lets me cry it out. His Wolf rubs against my mind and I let him in, replaying the awful fight from my perspective and reliving the whole, horrible experience of watching him fall, his belly torn open and feeling like my heart was breaking in two. The Wolf whines softly, encouragingly, and I let my memory sweep over both of us, letting him see what happened next. My fury and resolve. Opening the door I picture in my mind to contain the voices that follow me everywhere. How I used my gifts to destroy the Fae creature and heal his terrible wound. Tate gasps and pulls back enough to cradle my face in his hands and force me to look at him.

"Jesus Christ Ulla, *that's* what happened??" He asks. His frown is deep and worried. I nod, not trusting my voice to speak and not just keep bawling. I can feel my chin wobbling and I watch him as he strokes his thumb across my cheek, wiping away the tears streaking down my skin. He blinks once and then he crushes me to him, holding me so tight that I'm not sure if I'll be able to breathe, but I don't care because he's here and he's ok and I never want him to let me go.

"You're a Goddess, Ulla Mine," He whispers.

"Oh holy crap!" I gasp. The rest of my memories sweep over me and they tumble down the bond. I share them all with him. Of meeting the actual Goddess and the world that connects worlds and how incredible she is. How beautiful and powerful and real. I remember what she told me about my birth story and the choice she offered.

I show him everything, using my gifts for once and not shutting them down, deep inside of myself. It feels incredible, terrifying and electrifying all at once.

"You're incredible." He says into my neck. "I can't believe you chose this life with me over being a Queen."

"It was never a question. I'll always choose you." I hear him purring in his broad chest and I pull back just enough to be able to put my hands on his face.

"I love you, Tate, so much."

He blinks fresh tears out of his own eyes now and his smile shines like the sun. I smile back, and lean forward to kiss him. Softly at first, we press our mouths together, but within a few breaths we can no longer be gentle. The kiss becomes fierce and passionate, everything we feel for each other and the fear of what might have been, courses through both of us until we're panting into each other's mouths and we share even the air we're breathing. I slide my hips over his and push against him, needing to be claimed all over again. Needing to feel him so deep inside me that there's no question of where I am and where I belong. It's always been here, with him. He's my whole heart and I need him desperately. His hands are all over my body, sliding up and over my thighs and ass.

"Ulla, are you ok enough for this?" He groans against my lips.

"Yes, oh yes, are you?" I pull back just a little, looking into his eyes. His scar is so long, still so fresh.

"Gods yes, I'm fine, you saved me."

And then we're crashing back together again, grinding and moaning into each other, my hands still on his cheeks and his are kneading the flesh of my ass, spending sparks up my spine and over my scalp. I wrap one arm around his neck so I can pull him closer and rise up enough on my hips to center the tip of his cock at my entrance. I moan out loud as I slide down, the friction against my clit nearly sending me into a climax already. I'm so slick and he's so hard and everything feels *so right*. He pulls my ass cheeks wide as I slide down onto him, taking him all the way inside of me.

"Fuck, Ulla, I love you so much. I'm yours, always and forever." He grits into my ear. We move together, rising and falling as one, the tight slide of him inside me and the grind of our hips creates a swirling vortex of ecstasy that sweeps me under. I cry out, my body tensing in the throes of an intense orgasm. He bucks his hips hard up into me and chases his own climax while I come and come and come. I throw my head back and ride him as he stiffens under me, his release hot against my inner walls.

We're both breathing hard, coming down off of the intensity of such an explosion, a feat in itself. His thick length is still inside of me and I clench around him.

"Oh Gods, Babe, you're going to kill me!" He gasps, chuckling deeply. He kisses me all over my face and neck, our sweat-slicked skin pebbling from the air flowing in his bedroom window. I frown as I realize where we are.

"Have we been here at your place the whole time I was out?" I ask him.

He nods and continues to kiss me. Laying me on my

back and moving down my body as he pulls out of me. I feel the emptiness of his leaving and pout.

"Just for a little while, Love, I've got some worshiping to do."

I grin up to the ceiling and enjoy feeling his warmth over me.

"Desi was in the clearing when I woke up, or shortly thereafter I guess." He says. "She brought a backpack with snacks and once I got dressed we brought you here. You were out cold. Alma filled your parents in on an abbreviated version of what Desi had seen and they agreed that settling you in one spot to rest was the best idea." He pushes his weight down on my legs and settles his head on his crossed arms over my breasts.

"I was so scared." He confesses. I feel the corners of my mouth turn down and tears fill my eyes.

"You looked so small next to that creature and I couldn't stop my Wolf from getting in between you. When he sliced me open and I realized I couldn't protect you anymore? That was the worst moment of my life."

"Oh, Tate." I feel the tears falling down into my ears and I shimmy myself down so that I can look up at him. He lets me and we lay together, looking deep into each other's eyes for a long moment.

"But you didn't need me to save you," He whispers. He's looking at me with pride, wonder, and so much love, all swirling together in his eyes.

"But I do need you to love me," I say softly.

He smiles then, and kisses my nose, my forehead, then my lips.

"I love you forever, Ulla Mine." He growls softly into my mouth.

I kiss him back, sliding my arms around his neck and

pulling us as close together as two people can get. This man is my anchor in this world, a supportive partner and a smoking hot werewolf boyfriend. A girl could do worse!

The end.

The Bit at the Back

Thank you so much for reading Tate and Ulla's story! Do you want even more of these two and their shenanigans?

I've got a bonus epilogue just for you then!

Sign up right here so I know where to send it!

https://www.subscribepage.com/ewfbonusepilogue

Want to keep up to date with the rest of the gang in Eliza Falls and get updates on new stories and when fun new features are being released? Subscribe to my newsletter and never miss a thing! I've got some fun plans up my sleeve and I'll be telling my Newsletter Babes before anyone else. Keep your eyes on my website for updates, blogs and exclusive offers not found anywhere else!

www.maggiefrancis.com

Did you love Earth Wolf & Fire? I know you hear it all the time, but reviews really do make a major difference for us authors, please consider leaving a review so other reader

Babes can discover the fun of Eliza Falls! I appreciate every single one and it helps me tremendously. I'm so glad you're here!

May your tea always be hot and your cookies fresh,
    xox
    Maggie

Love Notes

This ridiculous book wouldn't have been possible without the help of a few rad babes in my life so I'm going to do that thing where I give them a shoutout to say thank you.

…

To the usual suspects, my husband and offspring, ahem, sweet cherub children: thank you for all of the love and support a tired mom could ask for and for not coming downstairs to talk to me until 7 am everyday. I love you guys.

To my Bookclub Babes and Beta team: How do I love thee? It's a helluva lot and I'll get weird about it if I think about it too long. You've seen this and know what it looks like. I'm sorry, but also NOT AT ALL.

To J.M: Your continued design help and sweet support has brought to life another excellent cover design and I can't wait to harass you for the next one.

To K.C: your belief and support in this dream has lifted me up and made a lot of it possible, thank you SO MUCH.

To S.H: You know that thing you do where you constantly remind me how awesome I am and generally cheer me on while I make weird, beautiful things? I really love that about you. Keep up the good work! I lurve you.

To my dreamy editors: You have made these rag tag stories into so much more than I could have on my own and I've learned so much already! THANK YOU.

To my Mom: Thank you for putting all those books into my hands over the years, for introducing me to Sci Fi/Fantasy in general, and *Buffy The Vampire Slayer* specifically. Buffy Night will forever be a formative experience for me and this adventure owes a lot of its inspiration to you. You done good.

To chocolate: Dark lover, I will continue to reach for you during all steps of the process to write, edit and generally continue these literary shenanigans with the pizazz that only you offer. I love you. Maybe more than I should.

If I haven't listed you here, it's only because I do a lot of my work at 5am and the hit of caffeine from my first cuppa hasn't hit that part of my brains yet. But I love you and appreciate you and I will stew in guilt and anxiety about it forevermore.

If you are still here, Sweet Reader. I love you too. xox

About the Author

Maggie Francis is a middle aged human who enjoys the cozy things in life; tea, books, warm socks and fresh bread, that kind of thing. She discovered long ago that getting lost in a book was a great way to spend time, and has since started creating her own world to get lost in. Eliza Falls is the joyful escape that she offers to readers, a place where magic is real, the heroines are kick ass, and the heroes are swoony.

Maggie writes steamy, paranormal romcoms from her little home office on the gorgeous west coast of Vancouver Island, on the ancestral lands of the Coast Salish, Songhees First Nation and Lekwungen speaking People.

Maggie eats too much chocolate, drinks a lot of tea and reads way more books than is reasonable for an adult person with a job and responsibilities.